"Let me get this straight. You want to create a sex scandal?

"And this scandal of ours—you want me to cover it in the *Louisiana Daily Herald?"* Zane continued incredulously.

Toni took a deep breath. "It might raise circulation."

Zane bit back a chuckle. Yes, increasing circulation was just what the paper needed right now. If she was right, and profits increased, no one would have to be fired, a task he knew his brother, Grey, had been putting off.

She cocked her head, then licked her bottom lip, possibly from nerves. Yet she seemed very sure of herself. The contrast intrigued him, almost as much as it confused him.

"So, do we have a deal?" she asked brazenly.

It was a good thing he and Grey had switched places, Zane thought. He couldn't imagine his conservative twin even considering Toni's bargain. On the other hand, Zane planned to enjoy himself fully.

"Exactly how far ... Zane asked, h...

Toni offe... ...nds on how inno...

Dear Reader,

When my good friend Julie Elizabeth Leto and I started working on the concept behind our linked stories, *Double the Pleasure/ Double the Thrill,* all we had was a vision for the cover—sinfully sexy twin brothers who share the same face. And then we played the "what if" game. What if those twins decided to trade places? And what if we set both stories so that the time line in each was running concurrently? And to top it all off, wouldn't it be cool if the books were published in the same month, placed on the shelves side by side, so that the two halves of the hero's face formed a whole?

Well, we've managed it. And while the writing of these stories has definitely been a challange, it's been a lot of fun, too! It's hard not to fall in love with the Masterson twins. Each is so confident, so cocky, so irresistibly sexy...and each gets exactly what's coming to him when one special woman crosses his path.

Although each book can stand alone, I fully believe you'll double your reading enjoyment if you get them both. Why settle for one of these delicious guys when you can double the thrill and have both of them?

Enjoy!

Susan Kearney

P.S. Check out my Web site at www.susankearney.com for news about upcoming releases.

Books by Susan Kearney

HARLEQUIN BLAZE

25—ENSLAVED

HARLEQUIN INTRIGUE

594—LULLABY AND GOODNIGHT
636—THE HIDDEN YEARS
640—HIDDEN HEARTS
644—LOVERS IN HIDING

DOUBLE THE THRILL

Susan Kearney

TORONTO • NEW YORK • LONDON
AMSTERDAM • PARIS • SYDNEY • HAMBURG
STOCKHOLM • ATHENS • TOKYO • MILAN • MADRID
PRAGUE • WARSAW • BUDAPEST • AUCKLAND

For Brenda Chin,
an editor who likes to buy new authors and new ideas.

For Krystyna de Duleba, a creative art editor
with a most excellent vision.

And for Julie Elizabeth Leto, friend and fellow writer
whose company I've had the good fortune
to enjoy for the past ten years.

RECYCLED PAPER

ISBN 0-373-79054-6

DOUBLE THE THRILL

This edition published by arrangement with Harlequin Books S.A.

Visit us at www.eHarlequin.com

Printed in U.S.A.

1

MAN, THAT SUCKER'S HUGE.

Toni Maxwell's mouth went drier than the New Orleans summer drought. She'd never expected anything so big, so in-your-face. But then how could she think straight under this kind of pressure? The never-ending heat wave must have fried her brain. Obviously, she'd been working too hard on her spring collection, because this couldn't be happening. Not to her. Not now. She had always expected to hit the big time—but certainly not like this.

Big was one thing. This qualified as enormous.

Toni's nerve endings danced with agitation and quickly repressed awe. She licked her bottom lip and told herself that she could not be intimidated. She would not say yes, no matter how enticing the offer.

Her inner voice egged her on. *Go on. Try it on for size.*

"I shouldn't."

Oh, pull-ease! Indulge.

Unable to resist the seductive temptation, carefully, Toni reached out, barely breathing, knowing it wouldn't fit.

It fit perfectly. As if custom-made for her.

"Awesome ring." Her oldest sister, Bobby, wearing pink running shorts, a pink sports bra and pink athletic shoes, jogged into the foyer swinging a two-pound weight in each hand and bouncing up and down on her toes as if fearing that if she rested for a second, she'd regain one of the thirty pounds she'd lost during the last year. "Hey, Mickey," Bobby yelled to their youngest sister in the kitchen. "You better come have a look."

"Did you break another nail?" Mickey yelled back, in her naturally sultry voice, the one that the broken-hearted men she'd refused to date often called just to hear on the answering machine. "We're out of pink nail polish."

"No, I didn't break a nail," Bobby replied, continuing to bounce and swing her arms. "Toni's getting married."

"What?"

"I most certainly am not," Toni contradicted, her stomach clenching in protest. She should never have opened the damn box in the foyer. After signing for Senator Birdstrum's present, she should have run up the stairs to her room where she could have had a little privacy, but she'd never expected an engagement ring—especially not after she'd repeatedly refused Birdstrum's proposals. For attending a fund-raiser with him on short notice, she'd thought he might show his appreciation by sending over her favorite chocolate pralines. But a four-carat engagement ring?

Why didn't the senator understand that no meant no? She gulped, attempting to swallow the lump of welling panic in her throat. And now, before she'd even recovered from her shock at his determination and fixation on her, she had her sisters to contend with.

The four Maxwell sisters shared the two-story house in the French Quarter. Expenses in this part of the city were high, especially for Toni, who had tapped out her funds to purchase the swankiest high-tech fabrics for her spring collection. But her new creations were sure to put her fledgling designer-wear boutique on the map and in the black—especially since several of the evening gowns had been featured in *Southern Design Magazine.* Her reckless decision to open her own business might soon pay off. According to the article, Toni Maxwell was "on her way," although her bank account didn't yet reflect her recent success. But she didn't live with her sisters just to save money—they also liked one another, most of the time.

Their personalities varied, from conscientious but sometimes rash Mickey to workaholic Toni to bubbly Bobby to Jude, the perennial student. All single, they looked out for one another in their own Maxwell way, which meant everything from blunt advice to shared clothing, comfort hugs, ice-cream binges on dateless Friday nights and elegant potluck dinners.

Growing up, Toni had seemed to be her parents' favorite, but her sisters didn't mind since she always worked harder than the other three put together. She'd studied long hours to make A's and B's all through school while working two part-time jobs, one as a retail store clerk, the other sewing clothes for family and friends.

But Toni could only remain serious-minded for so long before she had to blow off steam. This long period of sexual withdrawal was abnormal for her. Back then, as busy as she'd been, she'd still had time to indulge her passion between her busy days of hard work. Recently, her contacts with the opposite sex had dwindled to zilch, but she fully intended to correct her current predicament. She'd simply been putting in too many hours designing and selling her creations. All that work meant no extra energy to hook up with a man for even so much as a weekend fling. Her unconscious had picked up on her body's shortage of satisfaction, her mind taunting her while she slept with erotic images of a dream man, which had her awakening damp and slick. Self-gratification had barely taken the edge off her need for a man. She suspected the book she'd just read about actress Lane Morrow's affair with Grey Masterson, a New Orleans publishing tycoon had triggered the dreams. Wild dreams. Fantasy dreams.

So, she was eager to meet someone male. Someone hot. Someone who would make love to her for hours and make up for her abstinence. Someone like sexy Grey Masterson. Senator Birdstrum, too old, too stodgy, too bland, didn't fit the bill.

Dependable, hardworking, the one her siblings relied on when the chips where down, Toni could always count on her sisters to rally around her when she needed them. Back in high school on her prom night, her sisters had covered for her until she'd sneaked in through the three-story window at four in the morning. And they'd covered for her again during college when, on a whim, she'd accepted her French professor's offer to fly her to Paris for spring break. Between her sexual libido begging to be fed and her too-long-contained reckless nature primed for action, Toni wanted her sisters' input.

While Bobby might pretend to be enthusiastic about the engagement ring, Toni wasn't sure of her sister's true feelings. Toni had always suspected that Bobby harbored a bit of an infatuation for the senator, which Bobby vehemently denied. Still, Toni wouldn't hurt her for the world. But even if Toni was wrong about Bobby's feelings, she'd still refuse the senator.

What she needed right now was Mickey's cool-headed thinking. Her younger sister wouldn't be swept away by the romantic proposal from an old family friend Toni had dated exactly twice and whom she barely knew. The first time Birdstrum had proposed, Toni had been flabbergasted. When he'd told her she was the perfect woman for him, she'd been flattered, yet stunned. He'd stated his reasons that they should marry as if he were presenting a bill for a vote. She was beautiful, smart and well connected. He saw her boutique, Feminine Touch, as hip, her choice of career as clothing designer-retailer as the perfect way for her to remain busy while he worked in Washington. He'd given her logic—but no passion, something she most definitely wanted back in her life.

Her self-imposed celibacy made her now eager to end her exile from the male species. If Birdstrum was as sexy as Grey Masterson or her dream man, she might have been tempted to enjoy a fling with him. But there was no chemistry. No zing. Not even the tiniest arc of lust between them.

And as much as her life had been lacking in the sexual department, even she couldn't create fire without matches. She didn't mind starting the fire, but she needed a man who could fan the flames. A man creative in the sack, who knew how to excite a woman. A man as innovative and attentive as Grey Masterson had been in that bestselling novel. No wonder Lane Morrow's book had infiltrated her dreams. She'd denied an essential part of herself for too long, imprisoned herself in her career, and her subconscious was screaming for freedom. Satisfaction. Pleasure.

With her business going so well, she intended to take some time to appease her desires and find the zest missing in her life. Toni had no problem throwing herself into a romantic fling with the right man. She was young, single and enjoyed sex. While she might make her choices with a recklessness that made Mickey shudder, Toni's decisions had a way of turning out to be good ones. A new man in her life would replace her erotic dreams with stimulating reality. But first, she had to extract herself from her unfortunate situation with the senator.

With not even a droplet of attraction between them, turning down Birdstrum had been a no-brainer. And ever since he'd proposed the first time, she'd refused more dates with him and had let the machine answer his calls. Yet he'd continued to send her flowers and notes that repeated his offer of marriage. She'd never imagined he would buy her a ring, though. A four-carat diamond engagement ring! The man must be delusional to think she'd accept. It was downright scary to think that the senator enacted laws and represented his constituents so well when he had no clue about her non-feelings toward him. The ring was the last straw. It was time to put a stop to his antics.

Of all her sisters, Mickey would understand the cloud of trouble looming on the horizon and threatening to break over their heads like a deluge. Indeed, Toni could already imagine her eyes narrowing with some kind of scheme to get her out of this mess. A mess made even more potentially disastrous by the fact that it could involve their father, who wanted a job with Birdstrum.

Damn. Damn. Damn.

The two youngest Maxwell sisters might not look much alike, but they often thought alike. Toni was blond, average in height, slender with feminine curves.

Luckier Mickey oozed sex appeal, but didn't seem to know it. With her blond hair streaked naturally by the summer sun, a voluptuous figure and a brain that never quit, her sister was not only a man magnet—she possessed uncommon good sense.

Toni really needed some down-to-earth advice. Mickey glided into the room now as if she were walking down a runway, followed by the wondrous aroma of baking bread wafting through the air from the kitchen. Mickey was probably whipping up one of her wonderful Cajun meals, but she still managed to look pulled together in her hip jacket and slacks, likely bought at a thrift shop, and carefully protected from splatters with a funky apron.

Before Mickey could even look at the ring, never mind give advice, Jude rushed through the front door. "Those idiots called me a tree hugger."

"Well, you are," Mickey said, not unkindly, leaning forward to peek at the ring Toni held in her shaking fingers.

Jude was wearing jeans and one of her "Save the Gulf" T-shirts. As a full-time student and part-time lobbyist for several environmental groups, her lifelong cause—trying to prevent oil exploration in the Gulf of Mexico—had recently taken a back seat to lobbying for better protection of animals. Jude took in strays the way other women collected shoes. Thanks to Jude's charitable heart, the four sisters lived with an iguana, three cats, two dogs and a fish tank that currently housed a turtle.

Jude's flashing green eyes flitted to the sparkling ring like a honeybee to a gardenia, and she skidded to a halt, almost tripping over their white cat. "Oh, my. That's not costume jewelry, is it?"

"Senator Birdstrum's aide delivered it," Toni explained. At least with all her sisters here, she'd only have to tell the story once. Though, God knew, there wasn't much to tell.

"He sent someone else to propose for him?" Mickey asked, her perfectly arched brows drawing over a frown of disapproval.

"It's kind of sudden, isn't it?" Jude looked from the ring to Toni, then bent and scooped the cat into her arms.

"He won't take no for an answer."

"Typical man," Jude muttered.

Toni sighed. "And I only went out with him twice."

"You must have made quite an impression." Bobby giggled.

Toni could see by Bobby's expression that her sister thought she'd made love to the senator. Toni might have been working too hard this last year, but she had a reputation for having fun. And if a new guy she met had the right combination of intelligence, charm and sex appeal, Toni dived right into the relationship. So now explanations were in order. "We didn't have sex."

"It's been a while for you, hasn't it? You might want to try getting it on again sometime this millennium," Jude told her with a straight face, her tone sarcastic. "It's good exercise."

"Easy for you to say. You have a boyfriend."

Toni had been so wrapped up in the store she'd been on a sexual diet, and she missed everything about lovemaking. Touching and caressing. The scent of honest male sweat. The relaxation that came with losing oneself with another person. Good sex was like European chocolate, flavorful and yummy, and her mouth suddenly watered with a craving that she needed to satisfy soon. But she didn't want her sister's pity. "I've never really been interested in him. I only hung out with the senator at Dad's urging."

Their father specialized in drawing up budgets for the governor in the Department of Professional Regulation. But she well knew that he aspired to move to Washington, D.C., and work for the powerful Senator Birdstrum, head of the House Committee on Ways and Means. Her father's dream was one of the reasons she'd agreed to date the senator. However, this was one time she should have said no to a favor for the father she adored.

Toni might like to have fun, but she had her standards. The man had to appeal to her. From vivid descriptions in Lane Morrow's book, she could imagine indulging her desires with a man like Grey Masterson, but never with Birdstrum.

But how could she have predicted that Senator Birdstrum, who otherwise seemed normal in every way, would become fixated on her? Toni breathed in, then let out a frustrated sigh. "Apparently Birdstrum's been telling mutual acquaintances that we're engaged. I assured a customer just this morning that it was only a rumor."

"You can't marry him," Mickey told her.

Toni resisted swearing under her breath and petted the cat Jude held instead, but took little comfort from his warm purr of affection. "Of course I can't marry him."

Her sisters nodded, all three in agreement. Between the four of them, they would think of some way out that wouldn't jeopardize the family's interests.

Charming, arrogant and honest, Birdstrum was a capable senator. He also refused to accept her refusal to marry him. She'd already told the man no. She didn't know what else to do. Her father would never get the job he coveted in Washington if she dealt too harshly with the powerful senator. On top of that, Mickey could lose the cooking-school scholarship the senator had arranged for her, and Jude would lose her best lobbying connection.

The senator's diamond ring had come out of left field. And now she was in a real old-fashioned pickle. What the hell was she going to do?

Mickey led them all into the kitchen where they gathered around an antique table with four chairs from different periods from New Orleans's past, all covered with soft yellow seat cushions which gave the room a homey feel. After they'd moved in last year, they'd patched and polished the lovely mosaic tile floors, dark wood paneling, original ceiling medallions and refurbished the antique wood ceiling fan. From the kitchen they could see into the now darkened dining room filled with potted palms, a fluted iron post railing and flickering gaslights which they could turn on when guests arrived to show off the turn-of-the-century chandelier. But the sisters preferred to camp out in the kitchen where they could also look outside through beveled-glass windows to the draping weeping willow tree over their home's private courtyard.

There had to be a way to avoid the senator, but in her bleak frame of mind the only way out seemed to be to flee the state. In reality, though, she knew she couldn't leave her home. She loved living here and couldn't imagine just disappearing and giving up her home, her sisters, her business.

Mickey did most of the cooking, and the scent of

the bread she took out of the oven combined with the gumbo simmering on the stove normally made Toni's mouth water. But as one sister ladled soup and another sliced the warm homemade bread, her unsettled stomach warned her not to eat. Not until she figured out a solution to her dilemma.

"There's no avoiding the senator without leaving the state. But I'm not going."

Jude set a bowl of gumbo in front of her. "Why should you leave?"

"I'm not sure what else to do. Last week, the newspaper ran a small article about the senator's engagement. Although he didn't mention my name, that won't last long now that he's delivered the ring. I'm afraid of what he'll do next."

"Why don't you tell the newspaper that he's insane?" Jude suggested.

"I can't ruin his career just because he sent me a diamond ring. He's a good senator. And I don't want to hurt Dad's chances of getting the Washington job with Birdstrum."

Mickey poured lemonade, then took a seat. "Come on, eat. We'll put our heads together and think up a way out."

"Don't take this the wrong way, but why does he want you, anyway?" Jude asked.

Toni shrugged. "He thinks our family is solid, that my past won't embarrass him and because I have a hip career. He thinks marriage to me will help him attain the young votes in his upcoming election."

Jude swore, Bobby sighed, and Mickey shook her head.

Toni appreciated her sisters' support and suggestions—she did—but they weren't helpful. "If I make an enemy of the senator, my business will likely go down the tubes, too. Birdstrum has powerful friends, lots of influence in this city. If he puts out the word, women will avoid my boutique.''

Bobby tore off a piece of bread and dipped it into the gumbo. ''So if you can't refuse, then we have to think of a way to make *him* change his mind.''

Toni raised a questioning eyebrow. ''Not a bad idea coming from someone who only wears pink,'' she teased. ''But how do I get him to back out?''

Her sisters might squabble among themselves, but against an outsider, they pulled together. Unfortunately, they had yet to come up with a usable scheme.

''We could set him up with another woman,'' Jude suggested.

''I don't think so,'' Toni shook her head. ''The senator doesn't have feelings for me. Actually, I'm not sure he's capable of having feelings for anyone.''

''You could claim you're engaged to someone else and only dated the senator because you had a fight with your real love,'' Bobby suggested, hungrily eyeing the bread, but stoically denying herself.

''Who could I claim as a fiancé? Between coming up with new designs and opening the retail operation, I haven't dated anyone in the past year.''

''Two years,'' Bobby corrected, ''but who's counting?''

Toni restrained a frustrated sigh. One of the reasons Birdstrum wouldn't take no for an answer was that there was no other man in the picture. If her sisters were worried about the lack in her sex life, it must be really obvious. When had she stopped paying attention to men? She liked men and they liked her. Except for her recent drought, she'd never gone too long without some special man in her life. But compared to her sisters, she now lived the life of a saint.

Last year, Mickey's heart had been broken and she'd sworn off men, but she'd come in last week after a date with a happy grin and smudged lipstick. Jude had her steady guy, and since Bobby had lost weight, she'd been something of a party girl. Sure, they'd all gone through ups and downs with various men over the past few years, but Toni had been alone way too long. She needed to find a man. Needed to put energy into going out, looking good, having fun, working off some sexual steam. Toni was ready for a mad, passionate love affair, the kind that made her flushed with lust and lighter than air. But first she had to lose Birdstrum.

"What about Alan?" Mickey suggested. "His looks could make anyone jealous."

Alan had been Toni's high school sweetheart. Gorgeous but with no sense of humor, they'd both gone their separate ways after he'd taken her virginity the night of the senior prom. She hadn't planned on having sex that night, but her curious and reckless nature had taken over and she'd never regretted her decision. Alan had been sweet, careful and experienced. He'd shown her a very good time. "I don't think Alan's wife and two kids would appreciate him trying to act as if he's my fiancé."

"Okay, so Alan's not a good choice. What about one of your college boyfriends?" Jude suggested. "The redhead was cute."

"And he's unavailable. He's attending Stanford Law School." Not only had the redhead been cute and smart, he definitely knew how to please a lady. They'd met during a study session for history that had turned into a passionate all-nighter. Once again, she'd made a hasty decision that had turned out quite well. During the two years she'd spent with him, she'd matured into a woman who knew how to please herself as well as her lover. Ever since college, redheaded men always made her feel warm inside.

Bobby sipped her lemonade and tossed a napkin over the bread, probably so she didn't have to face temptation. "Paul Summers?"

"He went to Tibet to find himself and study with his guru." What Toni didn't mention, but hadn't forgotten, was that Paul's study of yoga had extended into the bedroom. He'd been a master of self-control, and she'd benefited both physically and emotionally from the experience.

"Steven Pascal?"

"He's gay."

"Kevin Mc—"

"Don't even think it." Kevin McPherson had made her pulse pound and her knees weak. They'd met in a bar after a football game. He'd been great in bed, but the Tulane backup quarterback's vocabulary had been limited to two things: football and sex. If he'd had a brain, she would have married him in a minute. However, she'd enjoyed their time together way too much to hold his lack of intellect against him. Toni held up her hand to forestall any further suggestions. "There's no one suitable from my past."

When she'd graduated college, she'd considered her social life normal. She'd never been overly concerned that she hadn't yet found the right man to share her life. Now with still another three years until she reached her thirtieth birthday, she had plenty of time to meet that special someone. And thirty was by no means her deadline. Toni knew what passion felt like, that heady, giddy, floating-on-air feeling, and she'd be damned if she'd settle for less than the best. She wanted a man who she could respect, a friend to share her life with, a lover to have blazing hot sex with, a soul mate to snuggle up to at night—unfortunately the senator didn't come close to her stringent requirements.

"How long until the senator returns to New Orleans?" Mickey asked.

Toni shrugged. "Why?"

Mickey grinned. "Well, what do politicians hate above all else?"

"Losing an election?" Jude guessed.

"Admitting to doing drugs?" Bobby added.

Toni frowned at Mickey. "Answering questions about adultery?"

Mickey's eyes sparkled with amusement. "Politicians hate scandals. If you create a scandal, you'll no longer be perfect in his eyes."

Mickey's idea had merit. Toni's hopes rose. All her life she'd played by the rules, been the good girl, the responsible daughter, the conscientious sister. She'd had several discreet flings but for the most part had reined in her reckless nature. But her method of dealing with the senator—up-front honesty—wasn't working. It was time to switch her modus operandi. "So what kind of scandal are you talking about?"

"To work in New Orleans, the scandal has got to be juicy," Jude chimed in.

"Oh, I like that, the hotter the scandal the better." Bobby sighed dreamily.

"One that won't hurt anybody," Mickey added.

"I've got it." Toni grinned with satisfaction, knowing her idea could get rid of the senator and accomplish her goal of jumping back into the dating scene all at the same time. "I'm going to create a *sex* scandal."

Mickey rolled her eyes. "Create a sex scandal? I thought you'd conquered your reckless streak. You'd better think this through with care."

"And just how are you going to create a sex scandal?" Bobby asked, her eyes glimmering with encouragement.

"I need to hook up with someone famous. Someone hot. Someone in the news. Get my picture taken with him."

"In bed?" Mickey asked.

"Only if I like him. A scandal is mostly innuendo and rumor and manipulating the press. I've just got to find the right man."

"Don't we all," Bobby muttered.

"Poor Senator Birdstrum," Jude said. "He won't know what hit him. When our Toni puts her mind to something, she always carries through."

Mickey grinned. "Yeah, and, amazingly, things always seem to work out."

"But I still need the right man." Toni glanced at page one of yesterday's newspaper, did a double take, then picked it up with triumph. "Someone like Grey Masterson."

"He's perfect," Jude agreed.

"Perfectly yummy," Bobby said.

Mickey grunted. "I just read that actress's book about him."

Toni grinned. "So did I. The man's nothing if not sexually creative."

Jude leaned over and stared at Grey Masterson's photograph. "I agree he's the perfect man for a sizzling one-nighter."

Toni didn't bother to contain her enthusiasm. ''Why limit myself to one night when I could have two or three?''

''But how are you going to meet him?'' Bobby asked.

''I'll have to get creative.'' At the challenge of arranging a meeting with the handsome newspaper publisher, excitement burned through Toni's veins like bubbling hot wine. She couldn't wait to make up for two years of sexual abstinence. She only hoped he was as sexy in person as he looked in the newspaper. She was going to have fun with Grey Masterson. Lots of fun. Hot, sweaty fun.

2

One Week Later

"A BEAUTIFUL WOMAN IS stalking you. And you're complaining? Did I miss something?" Zane Masterson spoke into his speakerphone, leaned back in his comfortable plum-colored leather sofa and imagined Grey, his identical twin, in a straitlaced navy suit with a traditional red tie choking his neck, sitting behind a cluttered desk and bristling with indignation. Grey didn't like Zane's teasing, which made irritating his big brother all the more fun. They might share identical DNA, they might look so alike that their parents, who had a fondness for Westerns, had had so much difficulty telling them apart that they'd mixed them up when naming them. But there the resemblance ended.

Grey was the older brother by two minutes. Those two minutes had thrust Grey into the seat of responsibility running the family business, the *Louisiana Daily Herald*, and allowed Zane the freedom to explore wherever his curiosity led him. Although the two men were very different, they shared that special bond that only twins seem to have. Zane and Grey knew one another so well they could predict how their twin would act in any given situation. Each of them was aware of what was important to his twin and knew one another's likes and dislikes. Happy to have nothing better to do at the moment than needle his brother, Zane clasped his hands behind his head and grinned.

"You don't understand." Grey used *the* tone. The tone that caused his reporters to scurry for cover. The tone that made his secretary cringe and that caught the attention of city leaders. From the mayor to the chief of police to the Historic Restoration Society, his brother had clout. What Zane didn't understand was why Grey was complaining to him.

While Grey was editor-in-chief of the city's second largest newspaper, Zane did a little of this, a little of that and lived off his real-estate investments in the up-and-coming Art District. If his investments didn't work out, he could always fall back on his trust fund, but, in fact, he hadn't touched that account in years. Their lives suited their personalities. Since the brothers had been old enough to understand that people couldn't tell them apart, they'd seemingly set out to establish their own identities. They'd even attended different schools. Grey went to prep school and then an Ivy League college. Zane barely made it through public high school and their father had to pull strings to get him into Tulane. Grey wore suits and ties and oxford shoes. Zane preferred the casual look, in the finest cuts and fabrics, of course.

Zane loved his extravagant and luxurious lifestyle and couldn't imagine a better existence. He enjoyed the company of good friends here in New Orleans and kept in touch with other friends in cities all over the world. He never tied himself to business ventures unless he could install an outstanding manager to shoulder the day-to-day responsibilities, leaving him free to drop and go at a moment's notice. He would leave on a whim to catch an eclipse in Fiji or watch a sunset over the Indian Ocean. The options of total and complete freedom fulfilled him. Despite his mother's occasional nagging for grandchildren, he didn't feel any compunction to alter his life.

He enjoyed playing the field, and while Grey had yet to settle down with a wife and kids, Zane was leaving the responsibility of carrying on the family name to his older brother. He just seemed so much better suited to the task. While Grey associated with the city's movers and shakers, Zane's friends were the jet-set crowd who partied until dawn. As kids, then teens and into college, they may have occasionally switched places on a lark, trying on one another's lives for size, just to stir things up, but the switches never lasted long.

Zane much preferred his fun-loving friends to Grey's stuffy ones. In fact, he'd occasionally been a bit concerned about his brother's stoic lifestyle, wondering if his brother would know what to do with a beautiful woman if she fell into his bed—but not recently. Instead of writing the news, Zane's ultraconservative brother, much to Grey's chagrin, had become big news.

Apparently, over the past year, his oh-so-secretive brother had been carrying on a relationship with Lane Morrow, last year's leading lady of B movies and this year's best actress Oscar contender for the summer's surprise blockbuster. He'd been proud to know Grey had had it in him. Then Lane had ditched Grey for her new leading man. As if suffering being dumped hadn't been bad enough, Lane had written a tell-all book that hit the *New York Times* bestseller list.

Zane grinned. Apparently, his brother was quite the lover. Lane had supplied lots of juicy details, and poor Grey had yet to recover from his newfound notoriety.

Zane made an effort to appear sympathetic. "What don't I understand?"

"In addition to being stalked by some lunatic—"

"She's crazy?"

"Well not certifiable, not according to my investigator—"

"You've had her investigated?"

"I wanted to know if she escaped from some mental institution before I decided what to do with her."

"Why do you have to do anything?"

"Because she's stalking me, damn it."

"What does she want?"

"I don't know—"

"Why don't you ask her?"

"—and I don't care. I have other things to worry about than women and their impossible desires."

"Not according to Lane's book," Zane teased.

"I'm surprised you actually read a book, brother," Grey muttered. "And, of all things, that damned piece of—"

"Did you really make love in the back of her limousine while your reporters waited to interview her?"

"That's private."

Zane chuckled. "No, it's public now, bro. Very, very public." He pushed a little more. "Even I haven't done it in the bathroom stall at Commander's Palace. All these years you've pretended to be so restrained, then I read in this book about—"

"Zane." Grey used *the* tone again. This time Zane heard the edge of anger. "If you're done having fun at my expense, I could use some of your expertise."

"I have expertise? Can't wait to hear in what."

As far as Zane knew, he was an expert of nothing. He dabbled, dallied, puttered, and he savored—especially the ladies. He liked tall women and short women, lean ones, curvy ones, quiet ones and not-so-quiet ones. He enjoyed them shy, and bold. He relished the differences, lingered over his encounters until boredom overtook him, and then he moved on to more interesting subject matter. As a consequence, he knew a little about a lot of things, but was master of none.

"Don't you have a private investigator's license?"

"The instructor was a knockout. The only way I could get close to her" and boy, had they gotten close, in the bathtub and on the kitchen table "was to take her course."

"Do you remember anything from the class?"

"She had the greatest set of—"

"Anything about the course material?"

"I passed the final, didn't I?" Zane said only somewhat indignantly. Grey sounded a bit rattled. And for a man who considered revealing emotions a weakness and who usually kept his feelings corked tighter than a bottled genie, this tiny sign of frustration was probably just the tip of some huge revelation.

"I suppose I can count on you, then."

"As good as counting on yourself," Zane told him. "We do have the same IQ."

"Yeah, but I actually use mine," Grey countered.

Zane grinned, knowing his next comment would rub Grey the wrong way, maybe even enough to get him to the point of this conversation. "*You* called *me* for help, remember?"

"Someone's sabotaging the newspaper," Grey finally blurted. "For all I know, it could be my stalker. Her name's Toni Maxwell. The newspaper's trouble started around the time of her arrival."

"So post a guard to keep her out," Zane suggested.

"I posted two guards, Zane." Grey's voice dropped as if he were strangling on the words.

"And?" Zane prodded.

"She managed to walk right past them—in a gorilla costume, no less."

"Excuse me?"

"You know, one of those out-of-work stage singers who embarrass people with stupid songs on their birthdays."

"Very clever." Zane laughed.

"Perhaps, but not funny."

"Right. Not funny." Zane almost choked trying to muffle another chuckle. "So what kind of damage did the singing gorilla do?"

"For starters, she stripped."

"Naked?" Zane could just imagine Grey's face going catatonic at the prank. He'd have given up a week's worth of parties to have been there.

"The security guards arrived before she took off much."

"Too bad."

Zane didn't understand his brother. Why couldn't Grey act like every other red-blooded American man and salivate at the sight of a woman stripping? Zane had read studies that men thought about sex on an average of every five to six minutes. As a man proud of his hedonistic and passionate tendencies, Zane figured the estimate of five minutes couldn't be normal. The truth must be closer to two or three.

"Here's the clincher, brother. While this Toni Maxwell entertained the office staff at my expense, someone poured oil into the ink. We had to reprint the entire run in the main press and hit the stands three hours late."

At the conclusion of his brother's story, Zane steered his mind away from the very pleasant thought of this woman stripping in Grey's office. While he probably indulged himself much more frequently than Grey, he could focus on business and put two and two together when necessary. "And you suspect Toni Maxwell was a plant? A distraction?"

"Well, she damn sure doesn't work for the local singing telegram outfits."

"You questioned her?"

Grey remained silent. Very silent.

Zane knew his brother well. "You want me to question her?"

"I don't have the time or the desire."

And Zane did—if he forfeited the enticing invitation from a very nubile southern charmer that he'd met last Saturday night to go sailing on Lake Pontchartrain. She'd promised him an afternoon of delights as a not-very-sincere apology for asking about his bank account. While she could live off her plump trust fund without lifting a finger for the rest of her life, she was quite the little mercenary, more interested in his wealth and his opinion of prenuptial agreements than in him. While her attitude mildly offended him, he hadn't intended to let her opinions interfere with his pleasure.

The only other obligation in his immediate future was to meet with Reina Price, a close friend and tenant of the house in the Garden District he'd inherited from his grandmother. Reina, European and exotic, went to the same parties as Zane and knew the same crowd of people. He thought of her like a little sister who usually was capable of taking very good care of herself. Over the years, they'd become good friends and never before had Reina asked for his help. He wouldn't abandon

Reina now, especially when she felt she couldn't trust anyone else with her problem. The jewelry designer wouldn't tell him much over the phone, so he'd agreed to meet her tomorrow afternoon.

When Zane remained silent, Grey gave him a business recap. "Circulation is down. Paper and fuel costs are on the rise. The union is giving my attorneys fits. I'm going to have to fire people who have worked for us for years. And to top it off, I'm handling the fallout from Lane's book. I can't deal with this woman stalking me, too."

"You need a vacation."

"Sure, I'll just take off and leave all these problems behind."

"Why not? All your troubles will still be waiting for you when you come back."

"Maybe you can go off and relax while the family business is falling apart, but I can't." Grey sighed. "Never mind, Zane. I'll handle this somehow."

"You always do," Zane agreed, but guilt stabbed him. Grey had run the family business for years while Zane had played and dabbled and loafed. Now that Grey seemed at the end of a fraying tether, Zane felt obligated to offer, "Why don't we trade places for a while?"

His brother didn't respond immediately, making Zane wonder if Grey was considering the proposal or rolling his eyes at his twin's foolish idea. "Oh sure, and let you run the place into the ground?"

"Hey, hotshot. Sounds as though you're going down fast anyway. This way, if we go belly-up, you can blame me."

Even if the family business declared bankruptcy, the brothers would remain solvent. With their investments diversified, they could weather any storm short of a class five hurricane. But their great-grandfather had started that paper and their grandfather and father had kept it going, if not always prosperous. To allow the paper to fail, without making some effort to save it, didn't sit right with Zane. While he'd always been quite content to let Grey have the prestige and the headaches, it was only fair to take a turn.

"I don't know if I should let you talk me into this."

That Grey would even consider his suggestion revealed to Zane that his brother really needed a rest. And a new challenge might do Zane some good. He'd recently found himself bored with this year's crop of jet-set divas and the latest out-on-the-prowl divorcées. Living in Grey's penthouse in the CBD—central business district—would be no hardship. Zane could use a change of scene and a challenge.

"It'll be fun. You'll get to be me," Zane teased. "Just think…sleeping in past 5 a.m., beignets and coffee at Café du Monde nearly every morning, licking powdered sugar off the fingers of—"

"I'll keep my licking to my own fingers, thank you."

"Oh, come on." Zane knew his brother thought him totally incapable of running the paper—a place he'd avoided all his life. But now he found himself curious to see if he could make a difference. "I'll liven up the newspaper. Besides, I do have that pesky little degree in journalism, and I've never gotten to use it."

"That's precisely my concern."

"Think. No more paparazzi chasing you for comments about your sexual exploits. No more whiny lawyers to deal with. No more headaches over paying the bills."

"You really want to trade?" Grey's tone softened to almost wistful.

They'd done it before, but not recently. Zane didn't bother to remind his brother that they'd never been caught. Not when they were twelve and Zane had run the mile to pass a phys ed test for his twin who had had the flu. Not when they'd been seventeen and Zane had gotten drunk backstage and Grey had taken his place in the high school play.

People rarely probed beneath the surface to inspect the differences that made each of them unique. In Zane's case, he had never spent enough time with any one woman for her to really know him, valuing his freedom too much to commit to one woman for more than a few months. And he rarely held still long enough for anyone to see beyond his good-time-boy image—so Grey could say or do whatever he wanted as Zane without fear of causing any damage. And as for Zane, he thrived in the midst of chaos and, unlike Grey, who so hated having his private life made public, Zane intended to take advantage of the publicity.

Several ideas popped into his head, innovations for the newspaper that he'd hadn't even known had been in his brain until now. He figured the *Louisiana Daily Herald* needed a little shaking up, and Zane was just the man to do it. But, he had the good sense to keep his plans to himself. He justified keeping his secret by trying to convince himself that if Grey knew his intentions, he'd never agree to a vacation.

Yet never had a man been more in need. While Grey had spent his life cloaked in conservative business and respectability, now the entire world knew that underneath the polished exterior, he was more like fun-loving Zane than anyone could have guessed. While

Zane had always wanted his brother to loosen up, he didn't want him to unravel. However, Grey would never release the reins of control unless Zane convinced him to do so.

"Hell, I can delegate with the best of 'em. You must have some competent employees, so I can't screw up too badly." Zane had no intention of simply delegating, but he hadn't spent thirty-two years trying not to be Grey without learning how his brother thought. He sensed him weakening and backed off. Too much pressure and Grey would turn stubborn. "I'll even buy a pair of reading glasses and wear them. But if you would just take off one day of work and go in for eye surgery like I did, I wouldn't have to bother."

"It won't hurt you to wear clear glasses."

"Fine. You just need to do one thing for me."

"What?"

When Grey asked the question, Zane knew he had him. "I got a call from a friend of mine, Reina Price—"

"Reina Price, the jewelry artist?"

"You know Reina?"

"We ran an article on her gallery opening last year. How do *you* know her?"

"We hang out. She leases two buildings from me and needs help with a business problem. If we switch, you'll need to fill in. Might not be easy. She knows me pretty well. I'm supposed to meet with her tomorrow afternoon."

"You'll have to go to the grand reopening of Club Carnal tonight."

"As if I wasn't going already," Zane muttered.

"Yes, but as me, you'll need to get there early, interview the new owner and perhaps a few patrons, then get out before things get too wild.''

''You mean interesting.'' Zane paused. ''For how long are we switching?''

''For as long as you want.''

''And you'll take care of Reina Price?''

''If you take care of Toni Maxwell.''

With pleasure. Zane looked forward to being stalked. And he most definitely couldn't wait to be caught.

''YOU'VE SCORED INVITATIONS to the grand reopening of Club Carnal?'' Bobby squealed, dropping the day's receipts on the checkout counter of Feminine Touch, Toni's dress boutique, now closed for the night.

The last customer had left hours ago. With the curtains across the front windows drawn shut, the shop had more the feel of a risqué boudoir than ever. A canopy bed covered with acres of white lace dominated the display where one frothy black gown called out ''buy me'' to customers. And buy they did. The display had cost a small fortune, but Toni didn't regret her reckless spending. In fact, she hoped that one of the major department stores might soon pick up her new dress line. Feminine Touch was slowly expanding from evening wear into sportswear and flirty beach attire, and soon lingerie, allowing her to indulge her sensual side.

Toni grinned at her sister's enthusiasm and offered Bobby an invitation. ''Grey Masterson's going to cover the grand reopening, and I'm going to make my move. I want you to come with me tonight.''

Bobby fisted her hands on hips swathed in pink chiffon. ''What's the catch?''

''You have to model my new beachwear.''

"Beachwear?" Bobby frowned. "Club Carnal is the hottest nightclub in the Art District. We need haute couture. Versace. Dolce and Gabbana. Pamela Dennis."

"Tonight, skin is in." Toni grabbed Bobby's wrist and tugged her toward the rear of the shop where she created and sewed her designs. Huge cutting tables and sewing machines dominated the middle of the workspace. Along the walls, on pallet racks, she stored hundreds of bolts of material in various patterns and colors in everything from cashmere and angora to less exotic but comfy cable-patch cottons to the latest high-tech microsuedes. In the very back, next to the heavy metal exit door, stood a rack of finished products.

She searched through the nighties and gowns until she found what she wanted. "For Club Carnal's grand reopening, the new owner's throwing a bubble party."

Toni carefully removed a hanger from the rack and thrust her latest creation, cloaked by a plastic green garment bag, into Bobby's hands. Eagerly, her sister accepted the offering and tore off the plastic to reveal a shimmer of pink.

"Wow!" Bobby reverently stroked the material, her eyes lighting with pleasure. "It's gorgeous, but way too small for me."

"The material is ninety percent Lycra. It's guaranteed to stretch, shimmer and sizzle. Trust me. That outfit will mold to every curve—and when it gets wet, it won't sag."

"Wet?"

"This is a bubble party. Bubble machines froth all over the nightclub. It'd be one big wet T-shirt party, if anyone is gauche enough to wear T-shirts." Toni shooed her toward the dressing room. "Try it on."

"Okay."

"There's a matching bikini bottom and a bralette sewn into the top. The effect is seamless. No distracting lines other than female curves."

"Sounds wicked." Bobby headed through the curtains toward the dressing room.

Toni had chosen her target tonight carefully, determined to create a scandal that would be a win-win situation for both her and her target. Grey's paper had once done a story on her boutique, and he'd sent a reporter who was wet behind the ears and had been eager to please. The woman had done a fine job, even using a color photograph to accompany the piece. So she had felt a little guilty sneaking onto his paper's premises in the gorilla suit to get past the guard he'd posted at the front door. She'd intended to do a sexy striptease to gain his attention. That idea had been half baked, reckless, she now acknowledged. She had to do better. But at Club Carnal, she could approach him as if they'd never met. While she wasn't quite sure how far she'd go to create a sexual scandal, so much of that would depend on Grey. His previous reaction had been annoyance, his approach to getting rid of her all too businesslike.

Still, Toni wouldn't give up on her target, not when he was *so* perfect. After Lane Morrow had publicly dumped Grey Masterson, Toni figured that a new affair with another woman could only bolster his self-esteem and enhance his public image. But stalking Grey Masterson had perks she hadn't considered. Not only was the man in the tabloids almost every day, but he associated with people who counted. People who got noticed by the press and had their pictures taken. If she played her cards right tonight, she might obtain some free advertising, especially if her designs showed up in tomorrow's paper. More important, word of her planned escapade might make it north as far as Washington...and Senator Birdstrum.

At worst, people in the club would notice her newest creations, and, if asked, she'd discreetly hand out business cards to steer customers to Feminine Touch. She'd designed Bobby's outfit in pink, but, for herself, had chosen a hot apple-red that made her feel both seductive and slightly wicked. Half party dress, half swimsuit, the ensemble molded to her bustline and waist then the skirt softly flared over her hips and ended provocatively just inches below the matching bikini panty. The concoction was absolutely perfect for tonight's party. And for attracting a man.

The outfit gave her courage to act more seductively than she normally would have. To her, the red design was the costume of a woman more brazen than she was. Now all she had to do was act the part.

While Grey Masterson hadn't found her irresistible in the gorilla outfit she'd borrowed from Bobby—who moonlighted for a local company—she hadn't expected him to call security to escort her from his premises before she could strip down to something more enticing. But then Grey had only reinforced her belief that he was a workaholic like she was. However, tonight, she intended to knock his socks off. Toni touched up her makeup, choosing cherry-red lipstick to match her dress, darkening and smudging her eyelids until her eyes looked big enough to capture her quarry. Grey would not escape her tonight. She didn't care if she had to fight off every woman in the place for his attention. She aimed to get her man.

And she very well might have to do battle for him.

Grey was gorgeous enough to be a model—not that she could imagine him doing anything so prissy. With his strong jawline, cutting-edge cheekbones and firm mouth, he was a man's man, a captain of industry, wealthy and respected. Lane Morrow's tell-all book about his sexual exploits had only lent another dimension to the man's already potent business allure.

After meeting him in person, Toni realized she'd underestimated his natural charisma. Grey had a manner of eclipsing those around him, not so much from his towering height or broad shoulders, but just by the sheer strength of his character. From his dark chestnut eyebrows, one shade lighter than the thick hair on his head, to his Paul-Newman-blue eyes that pierced straight through his reading glasses and had made her grateful for the gorilla mask, he'd commanded the air around him.

She'd hoped her singing gorilla striptease would intrigue him, but he hadn't stopped scowling for even a moment. Even a glower hadn't marred the perfection of his strong nose, high cheekbones and swarthy tan. But approaching him during business hours, in his territory, had been a mistake. The mood hadn't been set for romance. And tonight, they would be on equal ground.

She didn't intend to leave the party alone. Shoving her natural inhibitions to the back of her mind, she told herself she would succeed. In a much more romantic club setting, she would gain his attention—her first step in creating a sex scandal.

Closing her eyes, she visualized the evening exactly how she wanted it to end. With her walking out on Grey's arm, and reporters taking notice, the gossip reaching all the way to Washington and the senator. To succeed, she needed to create a stir.

But as she and Bobby exited the cab outside the four-story Club Carnal, the only thing stirring was her libido. Stalking Grey Masterson had brought out a side of herself she'd kept hidden too long. Instead of sitting back and letting her social life spin in nowhere land, she was taking charge. Ready for a change. Ready to allow a little passion and fun into her life. Ready to enjoy herself with a fling that would make headlines and cause the senator to ask for his ring back.

Most nights, there would be a block-long line at the popular club's entrance and a stiff cover charge. Tonight was by invitation only. Two huge bouncers held open the doors and checked their names off on a list.

Beside Toni, Bobby's eyes opened wide, and she craned her neck to watch handsome men and gorgeous women step out of shiny limousines, wearing designer beach attire. A few men started out the evening bare-chested, and Toni couldn't help wondering what Grey would wear. She licked her bottom lip a little nervously. Grey Masterson could wear anything he liked and still look like a dream man.

At the sight of a woman in two tiny scraps of lace and a thong, Bobby gasped. "We're overdressed, if you can believe it."

Toni handed their invitations to the bouncer, who wore a tuxedo sans shirt, and stepped inside. Despite the music, she kept her tone low. "There's nothing wrong with nudity, but the best strippers know that half the fun is in the tease, in the imagination. If you show everything up-front, you've got nowhere to go."

"Uh-huh." Bobby clearly didn't believe her.

At the cloakroom, they checked their shoes, then the

barefooted sisters flowed into the club with the other shoeless guests. The floors above had been gutted, leaving an open area that was four stories high. Music with a heavy beat bombarded their ears. Spinning metallic balls reflected shimmering lights over people dancing amidst waist-high masses of bubbles flowing out of a bubble machine overhead. Rubber matting protected the floors and walls from water damage. The famous erotic art of Club Carnal had been covered with special Plexiglas to protect the paintings and sculptures from the moisture.

The slippery floor, combined with the beat of the music, had the crowd on their feet, spinning and twisting and gyrating. Dancers threw handfuls of bubbles into the air, or onto their partners, or rubbed it over slick skin. The crowd was clearly having a blast.

Off to one side, the bar had standing room only. Bobby spotted a friend and took off with a wave, leaving Toni alone to hunt down her prey. She circled the dance floor twice, then waited at the bar in a crowd, four people deep, to buy a Hurricane. She handed out business cards to several women who stopped long enough to ask where she'd bought her dress—which was now quite soaked yet, thanks to Lycra, held its shape, just as she'd designed it to. She refused to dance with the men who asked, preferring to wait for the right opportunity.

There was only one man she wanted to dance with. And Grey Masterson didn't seem to be here.

Perhaps he'd arrive fashionably late. But he would come. The one time she'd been in his office, his schedule book had been open to today's date and she'd read that he'd scheduled an interview with the owner. So she'd begged one of her customers for invitations to be here, too. Although Toni found it a little difficult to imagine conservative Grey partying, according to Lane Morrow, the man knew how to show a woman a good time. And Toni couldn't wait to learn if the conservative New Orleans businessman could cut loose as Morrow had claimed in her book. Now that she'd left her store and ventured into the city's nightlife, her need to discover if Grey could turn her on had her eager to meet him. Morrow's book had revealed that, behind Grey's forbiddingly conservative tycoon exterior, a playboy longed to emerge. Morrow could have lied. And Toni simply might not experience chemistry with the man, but she was impatient to find out.

Knowing the evening was still young, Toni sipped her drink. She had found a spot where she could lean against the wall. She would be patient. And wait.

She didn't mind. She spent her time eyeing the clothing, the accessories. Tangerine was in. As were large-hooped silver earrings.

Finally, she spied Grey Masterson. Damn, he looked good in a black cotton scoop-necked knit shirt and black jeans as he said goodbye to a petite woman Toni recognized as the new owner of Club Carnal. But her gaze focused on Grey. He looked sexy. Very sexy. Since he was smiling right at her, with an almost predatory gleam in his piercing blue eyes, she hesitated only slightly before she scooped stray bubbles into her palm, then blew the bubbles in his direction, a blatant invitation.

3

ZANE REMOVED THE nonprescription gold-framed glasses spotted with soap bubbles and hung them at the neck of his damp T-shirt. After his interview with Club Carnal's owner, he'd intended to briefly scope out the action, then turn in early as Grey would have done. Zane, on the other hand, would have arrived at Club Carnal fashionably late and partied until the place closed down in the wee hours of the morning, then slept the next day until noon. Just the fact that he'd shown up precisely as the doors opened solidified his impersonation of his brother, particularly while around some of Zane's regular party crowd.

Though Zane took breaks from the frenetic pace of the jet-set lifestyle every so often, to travel leisurely or to enjoy the private company of a woman, he'd never missed his usual frantic lifestyle so quickly. He'd just spent his first day, ten long taxing hours, as the editor-in-chief of the *Louisiana Daily Herald,* and he supposed tomorrow would be no less draining than facing today's multitude of endless problems.

No wonder Grey needed a vacation. Between juggling the media circus every time he stuck his head out in public, the phone's constant ringing with requests for interviews about Lane Morrow's book, and keeping a constant lookout for the stalker and saboteur, getting any work done, actually running the day-to-day operations, had proved almost impossible. So had checking out the women who worked for Grey. He hadn't come across one unattractive woman all day, not that he'd been able to do more than take a quick look.

Zane had installed two private phone lines with unlisted numbers just so he could make outgoing calls, then he'd toured the building, paying particular attention to security, grateful for the course he'd taken not too long ago. He'd hired extra guards and spoken to his security chief about upgrading the alarm system. He'd seen no signs of Toni Maxwell and had returned to his office where a mountain of paperwork and twenty-two urgent messages had awaited him. In short order, he'd approved tomorrow's front page, and then had shown up here to cover the story of the grand reopening of Club Carnal.

And, finally, he'd come face to face with Grey's stalker.

The exhausting day of pretending to be Grey and dealing with one difficulty after another suddenly disappeared as he found himself getting his second wind. The thought of leaving and missing whatever his stalker had planned for him seemed intolerable. Totally unacceptable. All day, he'd waited for her to show. Now she'd arrived with a cryptic Mona Lisa smile on her lips, and he yearned to know what it meant.

Toni Maxwell carried herself with the posture of a queen. Straight back, head high, she nevertheless had a friendly look in her eyes—and enough curves to make any man happy. With the slick soap bubbles causing her skin to glisten, he had the strangest and most compelling urge to take her into his arms and dance close enough to feel her slick skin against him.

Perhaps it was the aura of mystery around her, but

he couldn't account for the almost overwhelming lust that struck him with the force of lightning.

What did she want?

From the report Grey had on file, Zane had immediately recognized Toni Maxwell standing by the wall—almost as if she'd been waiting for him. However, the picture he'd seen didn't have the same impact as a personal view. Toni's expression sparkled with an appealing mix of mischievous minx and coy tiger on the prowl. Her short dress revealed every inch of her toned and shapely legs and hugged every seductive curve. Her breasts were perfect, designed to entice. She'd certainly arrived ready for seduction. When she'd scooped up a handful of bubbles and blown them in his direction, he had a pretty good idea who was her target.

And he was more than ready to let her seduce him. For the first time today, he thought he'd gotten the better end of his deal with his brother.

Zane held his breath, willing this stalker to stalk, hoping with every beat of his heart that she wouldn't change her mind now. She didn't disappoint him. Holding her drink above the waist-high bubbles, she swayed across the dance floor, the entire time keeping her gaze locked on his. She possessed light, mesmerizing eyes, come-hither eyes, that somehow provoked and promised and piqued his interest.

While his male instincts were to meet her halfway, it took every measure of his control to remain rooted and wait for her to come to him. Grey had to be crazy to run from this mysterious woman who exuded sex with a capital S.

Zane knew many beautiful women, but few with such a sense of self as Toni Maxwell. She personified sexy confidence to the nth degree, as, without hesitation, she boldly closed in on him. And all he could think was *yes, yes, yes.* He couldn't wait to hear her first words, hoping her voice would prove as intriguing as the rest of her.

"I've been waiting for you," she admitted in a tone flavored with spice and as smooth as honey.

The implications of her statement rocked him back on his heels and he couldn't restrain a triumphant grin. A woman who had the confidence to admit that she was waiting for him indirectly implied that she was very sure of her own worth. He liked her boldness as much as the reckless gleam in her eyes.

Curious to see what she would say next, he countered, "You've been stalking me."

"Busted." She sipped her drink, not so much to delay saying more, but, he guessed, to call attention to her mouth. Glossy red lips, perfectly full and tempting, that left a smudge on the rim of her plastic cup. Full lips that curved upward enticingly as she slowly swallowed. Then, for emphasis, she licked her full bottom lip with the tip of her delicate pink tongue. Slowly, she reached out and placed the flat of her palm against his heart.

Her tone turned teasing. "Do I frighten you?"

"What do you think?" he countered, covering her hand with his own, locking her fingers in his. Warm and eager, she didn't act coy or try to resist. And yet he had the feeling his touch had more effect on her than she wanted to admit.

Was her attempt at bold seduction an act? Zane knew women quite well and, despite her outer attempts at boldness, he sensed she was holding back part of herself. And that quality made her even more intriguing.

Grey might have just dragged her over to security and had a lawyer slap a restraining order against her. But Zane knew exactly why *he* wouldn't. There was an old saying about keeping one's friends close and one's enemies closer. If this woman was his enemy, he could find out more by talking to her than by sending her away. Besides, he enjoyed the slick feel of her skin beneath his, the sight of her white flesh enclosed in his tanned fingers, and, most of all, the mingled heat of their joined hands.

And he wanted her with a lust that he fought to control. She exuded a chemistry that would have overwhelmed a less experienced man. The impact of her arrival had him intrigued by her mysterious boldness and his curiosity about her motivations upped the stakes.

She made no attempt to pull her hand away, but leaned closer, almost, but not quite, snuggling against him. She smelled of the bubble bath swirling around them and her own fruity perfume. And when she spoke, her tone was low, almost as if she intended her words to entwine around him and draw him closer into the net of privacy she'd woven in the crowded club. "Your heartbeat is rock steady. The rate slightly elevated. You could be frightened. You could be aroused."

Hell, with her standing as close as she was, it was only normal for his pulse to shoot up. He'd wanted to take her to bed from the first moment he'd seen her across the room. Up close, she was even more delectable.

When he spoke, his deep voice more than matched the huskiness of hers. "So, are you going to answer the million-dollar question?" he asked into her ear, casually watching her to catch her reactions.

She chuckled and faced him squarely. "Which is?"

"Why are you stalking me?"

She raised one eyebrow. "You're a very attractive man."

He peered into eyes so full of amusement that he had difficulty believing she could be part of a conspiracy to sabotage their newspaper. However, she *had* sneaked into Grey's office while someone else had ruined the ink. The cost of reprinting had been enormous. Had she acted as an accomplice by creating a diversion?

"You're stalking me because of Lane Morrow's damn book, aren't you?" Zane guessed, watching her closely for the tiniest exhibition of guilt.

"Absolutely," she baldly admitted with no hesitation, not even a flicker of indecision.

He believed she'd just told him the truth. Odd how her admission shot a charge of excitement right through him. This woman was playing a game, but only she knew which one. And only she knew the rules. What did she really want? And why had she chosen Grey?

What did the book have to do with her presence here? Did she need some stud to make her happy? Or could she be one of those women who notched their bedposts with every celebrity that they conned into it? She didn't seem the type. So confident. So together. None of his former suspicions seemed to match Toni Maxwell in the flesh.

However, just because she claimed she was here because of the book didn't mean she was telling him the truth. He needed more information, much more information. For a moment, he entertained the thought of spiriting her away to a private nook, teasing her, taunting her, keeping her on the razor's edge of sexual desire until she told him exactly what he wanted to know. She wouldn't give in easily—which would make the rewards all the more pleasant. But he didn't want to frighten her away, so instead he hid his thoughts and spoke mildly. "You shouldn't believe everything you read."

"I don't." Again she surprised him. "It's the appearances that count."

"Would you care to elaborate?"

"I'm in the fashion business, which is all about appearances. The power of fashion is that it allows people to imagine they can be completely transformed by a gown, a bag, a pair of shoes or a diamond ring."

Her insight fascinated him. "And exactly what is that little number that you're wearing supposed to tell me about you?"

"Ah, I designed my dress with an evening like this one in mind." She cocked her head, her eyes daring him, challenging him. "Red is bold and symbolizes bravery. And lust. The thin spaghetti straps suggest fun. The snug material evokes the hidden desires inside the feminine heart."

"In other words, you designed the dress not to please a man, but to make a woman feel good about herself?"

She gazed around the dance floor, her intelligent eyes taking in first one woman's attire, then another's. All the clothing, men's and women's, was now soaking wet from the endless supply of bubbles. A few of the women, those who'd worn swimsuits over toned and tanned bodies, appeared attractive. Most looked disheveled, their wet clothes sagging and wrinkling—not that the men seemed to mind.

She turned back to him. "My customers are women. I know what they like by what they buy."

"How do you know women don't buy your clothing in the hopes of snaring a man? Or to please a lover?"

"Some do," she pleasantly agreed with him, her eyes sparkling. "But the smart ones dress to please themselves. Don't you?" She didn't wait for his response. "You're wearing all black, the color of power, the color of night. It's dark, mysterious, as if you have something to hide."

Were her words simply a coincidence? Or did she know his brother well enough to speculate that the twins had switched places? Did she even know that Grey had an identical twin?

Zane had worked with Grey's employees all day long, and no one had even suggested he wasn't his twin. Supposedly, this woman was a stranger who had only met his brother once. She couldn't know him well.

But, for all Zane knew, she could have been secretly stalking Grey for years, and only recently decided to so boldly come forward. According to her file, Toni Maxwell had no history of mental illness. He, a connoisseur of women, found her mentally stimulating, physically attractive. She seemed just as sane, maybe saner, than anyone Zane had met in years.

But, she deftly kept turning the conversation away from herself and her purpose and back to him. He didn't particularly want to know what his choice of clothing revealed about himself. Especially since he'd had to search hard and long through Grey's closet to find anything suitable for the opening of a hot nightclub. He was much more interested in her and her reasons for stalking him.

"So women buy clothes to project a certain image—

an image that may not be true?'' he asked, keeping up his end of the conversation.

She lifted one delicate shoulder in a shrug. ''What is true? I believe truth is what we perceive. And what I perceive and what you perceive may be very different.'' She gazed upward to one of the enormous erotic sculptures hanging high above the dance floor. ''What do you see?''

The couple entwined in an embrace of smoked glass were naked. ''I see a couple about to have sex.''

''I see a man and woman in love.''

''Our two thoughts aren't mutually exclusive,'' he mused.

''You noticed?'' she teased.

He knew love existed. Just like he knew that if he jumped off a skyscraper, he would die. Thankfully, he didn't need to personally endure either experience to accept the reality. ''So you're saying it doesn't matter if what's written in Lane's book is the truth, as long as everyone believes it's the truth.''

''Exactly.''

''I'll be damned. My sexy stalker spouts philosophy.''

She chuckled and kissed his cheek, her lips as soft as a rose petal. ''I'm Toni Maxwell. Pleased to meet you, Grey.''

Toni probably had no idea that his twin had investigated her, that Zane had known her name before he'd set eyes on her or that he had no intention of telling her about Grey's investigation. He wanted to see if she would lie to him. So far she hadn't, although she'd most skillfully avoided answering his primary question. Why the hell was she stalking Grey?

He tried again, shifting from one foot to the other. "What do you want from me?"

"Your time."

A flattering answer, but too vague to mean much. Earlier, she'd said she was here because of the book. But she didn't necessarily believe what she'd read in the book. Confused, but fascinated, he found himself enjoying their banter and her company much more than he'd expected. And he couldn't quite figure out why he was responding so strongly to her. He didn't usually have such a surging swift urge to back a woman against a wall to ravage her mouth. He considered himself civilized and in control of such primal urges.

Yet, he wanted a taste of Toni Maxwell's lips more than he'd wanted anyone's in a very long time. He didn't understand the powerful pull she had on him, but, as usual, he went with the flow, sensing they could have a very good time together.

But he had to kiss her. Soon.

Thankful for the tight jeans that kept his arousal tamed, he shifted to his other foot in search of a more comfortable position. Toni Maxwell was one mystery he would enjoy solving.

Testing her, wondering just what she wanted from him, he took her drink from her hand, allowing his fingers to slowly graze hers, before he lifted her glass and sipped, an intimate gesture between strangers. The pulse at her neck fluttered and her pupils dilated slightly, causing his breath to hitch.

He had to kiss her. Very soon.

"It's good." Her drink tasted of fruit punch and possessed only a touch of dark rum, as if she'd ordered the drink mild. But there was nothing mild about the daring look in her eyes, which inflamed his own senses.

He took in the graceful arch of her neck, the bold curve of her breasts, the flat span of her waist, the flare of her hips and longed to trace his fingers along her flesh.

He had to kiss her. Now.

She leaned against him and wrapped her arms around his neck. Tilting back her head, she peered straight into his eyes, then tugged his head to hers. "If you wanted a taste of fruit punch, there's a better way to—"

Finally, he kissed her, expecting the fierce passion of locking lips and the exploration of entwining tongues, but, again, she surprised him. She parted her lips only very slightly. Instead of an open invitation, she lured him with delicate nips and nibbles, keeping their kiss light and superficial before pulling back with a satisfied smile that left him thirsty for more.

She sipped her drink, offered him another swallow, then demanded, "Dance with me."

She tugged him away from their partially private spot by the wall and deposited her almost empty cup on a table. Together, they entered deeper into the froth of bubbles and the anonymous dancing masses.

Zane realized that meeting her and talking to her had triggered the familiar passionate responses in his body. His heart rate was up, his flesh warmer than usual. Despite his long day, energy zinged through him. Sleep was the last thing on his mind—unless it was sleeping with Toni. But however familiar his physical response, the unfamiliar mystery surrounding this woman made him wary, but it also added a certain tangled excitement to the mix. The element of peril had triggered unusual reactions. He felt more alive, more awake, more interested than he'd been in a very long time.

Instinct also alerted him to danger. Not that she

could be hiding a weapon under that skin-hugging red dress. He wasn't worried that she might suddenly attack him, but rather that she had sneaked through his hardened defenses. He liked her. He liked her quick wit. He liked her intelligent femininity, so different from the mercenary women he usually met, women more interested in his pedigree or his bank account than his thoughts.

He sensed Toni wanted more and wouldn't ever settle for less. He just couldn't figure her angle. She was a businesswoman with a unique outlook on life that he couldn't categorize. He still didn't know why she was here, but right now he was almost pleased she hadn't revealed her secret. Now, he had a reason to spend time with her, pursue her.

She danced provocatively, her hips moving to the beat, her upper torso undulating with a natural rhythm. And he sensed that, while she knew exactly how attractive he found her, she moved to please herself. As she spun around, her skirt flared, and he caught sight of her panties, the legs cut high enough to tease, the Brazilian bottom brief, snug, deliciously enticing in the way the fabric molded to very sleek, taut curves.

Her skin glistened with bubbles, drawing attention to the delicate arch of her neck, the soft curve of her shoulder, the shadowed cleft between her breasts. But her face, so full of fun, drew his eyes like a magnet. Her blond hair, damp from the bubbles, was slicked back to frame high cheekbones and glossy red lips. A no-apology gaze penetrated his defenses. No matter how he moved, no matter who jostled them, she focused on his eyes, her gaze hauntingly intimate. Mesmerizing. Tantalizing.

One moment her eyes looked blue, then green, then

gray. In the swirling and flickering lights, he couldn't tell their color. She presented one tempting challenge. There was so much more he wanted to know about Toni Maxwell. Like the taste of her tongue that she'd held back during their kiss. Like the feel of her curved bottom that he didn't dare yet touch. Like the words she'd murmur when they made love. And he intended to make love to her. All of her.

He swallowed hard. The bubbles that clung to his clothes had popped, leaving his T-shirt and jeans damp, but the dampness couldn't cool the heat rising inside him. As the tempo increased, they whirled faster, more frenetically, under the spinning neon globes.

He lost track of time. He forgot why he was here. Although the crowded room was full, it seemed as if there were only the two of them. Him. Her. And the bubbles flowing between them, keeping them connected, always connected. And when her hand brushed his hip, when her thigh grazed his, he knew making love to this woman would be pure magic.

He ached to sweep her upstairs to one of the semi-private balconies, but he didn't want to break the mood. This dance was like foreplay, and his anticipation rose. He reached to bring her closer and steal more than a fleeting kiss, but on feet that deftly spun away, she evaded him with a teasing gyration that took away his breath and left him aching, wanting more.

Through the rudimentary beat of the music, Toni had raised the stakes. Her dancing provoked an elemental and savage need in him, to grab her, to take her, to make her his, if only for a few short hours. Ten thousand years of civilization prevented him from acting on savage instincts.

It wasn't easy to overcome his arousal until Zane

remembered he was supposed to be Grey. Grey, who would have left hours ago. Grey, who wouldn't have spent the evening dancing in bubbles with his stalker. This irresistible attraction to Toni was going to make continuing his own agenda a little tricky, but not impossible. If they stayed much longer, Zane might even blow his cover. It was time to leave, only little miss stalker was coming with him.

"LET'S GO OUTSIDE for some air," Grey suggested, taking Toni's arm and leading her through the hip-deep bubbles to the foyer where they both retrieved their footwear.

Maybe fresh air would clear her head. She hadn't been prepared for the all-consuming attraction of Grey's magnetic blue eyes or how much her fingers itched to thread their way into his curly hair and yank his head toward her for a kiss. Back in his office when she'd worn the gorilla suit, he hadn't seemed the least bit interested in anything she'd had to offer. But tonight had been like lava spouting from a volcano, primitive, powerful, poetic.

She had to keep her priorities straight, though. This was supposed to be a sex scandal. A fling. And this was going to be a great fling, she could tell by the molten chemistry erupting between them. Toni adored being around beautiful materials, clothing and things. But being with such a beautiful man turned her on even more.

She had no idea where he'd originally intended for them to stop and rest their weary bodies, but when they stepped outside, photographers' flashbulbs popped in their faces. Blinded by the glare, her knees unsteady after the dancing, her nerves rattled by the evening, she hung on to Grey for support.

Which automatically played right into her scheme. The outraged senator would read the publicity in the papers and break off his pursuit of her. So she welcomed the paparazzi's taking pictures of the two of them together for her sake and for Grey's, too. His reputation would soar. The press could no longer write stories about him sitting home alone, pining for his actress. So far, her plan couldn't have worked better. Although she felt slight pricks of guilt for using Grey Masterson to achieve her goals, he could certainly look after himself. And this publicity could only enhance his stature as a man about town.

Besides, although she'd been willing to do so, she hadn't had to fake her attraction to him. After all, what was not to like? Grey was charming, attentive and fun. He'd seemed amused that she'd stalked him—not the least bit angry or annoyed like he had that day when she'd shown up in the gorilla suit. A little time gone by had apparently allowed him to find the humor in the situation.

And now with the photographers' flashing lights in his face, he slung one arm over her shoulder, protecting her from any reporters who ventured too close. She thought he might be annoyed by the attention, but he seemed more amused.

"Who's your date, Mr. Masterson?"

Grey spoke firmly. "Give her a break, guys. Stand back, and I'll answer a few questions."

His grace surprised her until she remembered that he was accustomed to dealing with reporters.

"Have you recovered from your affair with Lane Morrow?"

Grey glanced down at Toni. "What do you think?"

A woman stuck a microphone into Grey's face. "Are Lane Morrow's statements in the book true?"

Grey grinned. "Next question?"

"Are you going to write a book?"

Grey started walking through the gauntlet of reporters. "I'm in the legitimate newspaper business. And we verify our facts before we print them."

"So you're not going to let the world know that Lane Morrow is really a Martian?" teased one of the reporters.

"No comment," Grey said, avoiding the trick question and signalling for the valet to bring up his car.

Toni realized the danger. If Grey had answered by saying Lane Morrow wasn't a Martian, the headline, Lane Morrow's Ex-Lover Says She Isn't A Martian, could have showed up in tomorrow's paper. He'd wisely answered no comment, but that didn't mean these people wouldn't resort to putting words in his mouth. She only hoped one of them was smart enough to figure out her identity and print her name in the paper, preferably with her picture.

Grey's large tip was enough incentive to have the valet pulling his silver Mercedes up to the curb in a matter of seconds. Amid more popping flashbulbs, Grey opened the passenger door for her, walked around the front and then slipped into the driver's seat.

Toni had not agreed to go anywhere with him. But under the circumstances, discussing possibilities on the sidewalk was impossible. Toni had willingly gone along, knowing her sister Bobby wouldn't be worried by her sudden departure. After all, she'd known the plan from the start, a plan that had succeeded beyond Toni's wildest expectations.

One shared drink, several dances and stimulating conversation had set her scheme in motion. She settled into the cool leather seat, grateful that Grey hadn't turned on the air conditioner or complained about their damp clothing pressed against his expensive seats. He'd been quiet since closing the door behind the reporters, not saying a word about where he was taking her.

But she didn't worry much about their destination. A larger question loomed in her mind. She'd been working toward this moment since she'd seen Grey's appointment book and acquired the invitation to Club Carnal's grand reopening. Now that it was time to take the next step toward passion, she found herself out of practice and a bit hesitant of following through with the events she'd placed in motion. Sparks had sizzled between her and Grey, an unexpected bonus that had left her edgy and excited with her success. But now she had more decisions to make.

Just where did *she* want him to take her? And what exactly did she want to happen once they arrived?

4

ZANE HADN'T YET MADE ANY plans beyond escaping the paparazzi. He'd simply been grateful his jeans hadn't been bulging as the photographers had snapped their pictures. While he still craved to take the luscious Toni Maxwell to the nearest private spot and conduct a mutual exploration fest, he had himself under some measure of control.

So when Grey's car's cell phone rang, he almost spoke normally and with barely a trace of the husky sexual overtone that hummed through him. Wondering who would be calling his brother at this time of night, he hit the answer button and spoke into the speaker. "Hello?"

"Mr. Masterson?"

"Yes?"

"This is Officer Fugate, New Orleans Police Department." Zane's first thought was for his brother. Had there been an accident? His heart tripped, and he gripped the padded wheel hard enough to feel the steel beneath, waiting for the police officer to finish speaking. "We have evidence of criminal activity at the *Louisiana Daily Herald*'s distribution center."

The words soothed Zane's nerves like an easing balm. His brother was fine, probably sleeping in Zane's apartment.

But other employees of the firm were at work. ''Officer, has anyone been hurt?''

''No, sir.''

''What kind of criminal activity are you talking about?'' Zane asked, relief washing over him this time because there were no injuries.

Beside him, Toni seemed to be holding her breath—out of concern? From the moment he'd met her, she'd been so animated and alive, vivacious. But silent and still, she allowed him to see not just her true beauty, but to appreciate how she seemed to think before she acted. Toni Maxwell used her head. When another woman might be demanding answers, she'd had the sense to remain quiet while he questioned the policeman.

The officer spoke firmly. ''I realize it's late, but we'd appreciate it if you could come down and speak with us in person.''

''I'll be there as soon as possible.''

After Zane disconnected the call, he took a moment to assess the situation. This time of the evening, far from Bourbon Street and the late-night jazz sessions in the French Quarter, the streets in the Art and Business Districts were empty. He drove past plazas, squares and parks sprinkled among the commercial high-rise buildings and elegant luxury hotels, thinking about his next move.

Next to him, Toni remained quiet, so quiet that he had absolutely no idea how the news had affected her. She might have been surprised or had simply remained silent to let him deal with the problem. Or she could be covering up satisfaction that the paper had taken another hit. If she hadn't been distracting him this evening with her intelligent conversation and her alluring moves, he might have returned to the offices as Grey frequently did to catch up on paperwork. Had Toni been at Club Carnal tonight simply to keep track of Grey, so that her cohort could cause trouble at the office? Had their entire conversation and her interest in him been feigned so he wouldn't suspect her complicity? He believed himself a man experienced enough with women to tell the difference between genuine interest and the fabricated kind. She'd been interested. Her breath had hitched right before their kiss and her pupils had dilated—reactions hard to fake.

And while he wasn't so far gone in his lust not to have noticed that she'd been just as turned on by their meeting as he'd been, he still couldn't discount her as an accomplice. Maybe she got turned on by fooling him. And maybe he was fabricating farfetched plots where none existed. But, if so, then why had she been stalking him?

Zane figured that keeping her with him might be the best way to judge whether or not she had anything to do with the *Herald*'s problems. If she was involved, maybe she'd slip and reveal something she shouldn't. He told himself that's why he wanted to keep her with him.

Yet he couldn't deny that the problem at the newspaper felt oddly personal, as if he himself had somehow been violated. Zane's almost overpowering need to find Grey's enemy and protect the paper surprised him. He had to fight the urge to step on the gas and speed toward the *Herald*'s office. For a moment he debated if he should call Grey, and finally decided to make that decision after he'd spoken with the police. Grey needed a break from the stress, and Zane should be able to handle a small crisis.

Even if the woman sitting next to him was at the core of the problems at the paper, Zane was determined to solve the mystery around her. While Toni obviously had a high intellect and a fabulous body, she seemed stable and down-to-earth. Yet, she was also full of contradictions that both intrigued and fascinated him. He reminded himself that normal women didn't stalk men and then admit it. He reminded himself how often she'd evaded his questions. But what he remembered most was her tauntingly provocative kiss and the way her face had lit with amusement when she'd teasingly pulled back, even as her eyes had sparkled with silent promises.

Damn it. There had to be other suspects with a motive to harm the paper. A disgruntled employee or ex-employee? A rival competitor? Or was the attack more personal? With the stories the paper printed, Grey could have pissed off innumerable people. His reporters might have offended any number of crackpots or criminals. However, the most pressing question on Zane's mind was about Toni. Had it simply been a coincidence that tonight, as they'd danced, someone had harmed the paper? And if so, then she had another reason for seeking him out. But what?

The only reaction of hers that had seemed slightly off kilter was her lack of surprise at the photographers and her willingness to have their pictures taken together. Was that so she'd have an alibi? Or did she crave publicity?

Questioning but careful to hide his curiosity, he turned to Toni. "Sorry. This is not exactly the way I'd intended our evening to end. There's a problem at the *Herald*. Would you like me to drop you off?"

"No need to apologize. It sounds as though they

need you right away. Just drive straight to the *Herald.* I can always take a cab home.''

She sounded reasonable, practical and, damn her, not the least bit reluctant to end their night together. Was his suspicion too far-out that her offer to accompany him to the paper might be so she could find out how much damage her partner had done? Could a face that stunning bide a mind that devious?

It took a considerable amount of control to repress the powerful urge to stop the car, sweep her into his arms and kiss her senseless. A most un-Zanelike reaction. While he adored women, his reactions weren't usually this intense. Trading places with his brother had caused some almost overpowering emotions to surface—emotions he had no time to coddle.

He turned right at the next corner. ''Not every woman would be this understanding.''

''You're forgetting I'm a businesswoman. I know what it's like to put my capital, my time and effort and my dreams into a business. I'd be a wreck if anything happened to Feminine Touch—''

''Who?''

''Feminine Touch is my boutique.'' She twisted in the seat and placed a comforting hand on his shoulder. ''You have insurance?''

Her question put his suspicions back on alert. Why would she ask about insurance when they did not yet know the problem? Criminal activity could be anything. Graffiti. A bomb scare. Perhaps the silent burglar alarm had signalled the police, and they'd arrived before anything could be stolen.

However, her statement as well as the hand on his shoulder could also be perfectly innocent. Theft and arson, even flooding, would be covered by insurance.

But even if they had no insurance, he wouldn't reveal a potential weakness to a woman who could be his enemy.

"Our policy is so complicated that it takes a lawyer to decipher the fine print," he told her.

She accepted his answer with seemingly no suspicion. "What's the distribution center?"

"Where we load the delivery trucks. The fenced parking lot is behind our offices and patrolled by a security guard and two German shepherds," he revealed, knowing that information was easy to come by.

She didn't say more, and five minutes later, he pulled around back to the gate. Trucks that should have been on their delivery routes half an hour ago remained in the area. The vehicles were silent, the engines off, their drivers speaking among themselves in low murmurs. And there was no sign of the dogs or the security guard.

Even in their damp clothes, the night air remained warm. Still, Zane noticed Toni shiver as they exited the car. He reached into the trunk, removed a sports jacket and slipped it over her shoulders.

"Thanks."

Taking her hand, he approached the uniformed police officer who stood near the back fence, shining a light on an opening that shouldn't exist. The chain-link fence with barbed wire strung across the top had a triangular slice cut out, large enough for a medium-size man to slip through, showing quite clearly that an intruder had broken in.

"Officer Fugate? I'm Grey Masterson. And this is Miss Maxwell. What's happened?"

"It looks like someone broke in by cutting your fence, then vandalized your fleet."

Zane frowned at the silent trucks. "What was done to them?"

"Your drivers believe someone poured sand in the gas tanks."

"All of them?" Toni asked, her eyes widening as she gazed over row upon row of parked trucks.

"Your foreman told me that after several trucks' engines went dead, he ordered the others turned off—to prevent more damage."

"Where's the security guard?" Zane asked the foreman who came up to join them.

"We haven't seen him, Mr. Masterson."

"The dogs?"

"Gone, too."

"I tried calling the security guard's house. There's no answer."

"We sent an officer to the premises to question him," the cop told Zane. "The house was empty."

"You mean he wasn't home?" Toni asked, looking as puzzled as Zane felt.

"No, ma'am. The house was vacant. A neighbor confirmed that he just moved out."

"Who does the security guard report to?" Toni asked.

Zane didn't have a clue and made up an answer. "Administration. It's possible he called in sick, but it's also possible the guard was in on the vandalism," Zane muttered. "I'll leave finding and questioning him to you, Officer. In the meantime, I have a paper to get out."

He turned to the foreman. "Wake up every mechanic and get them in here. We'll need to drain the tanks, clean the filters. In the meantime, I'll see about renting us a fleet of vehicles. The papers might be late, but they are going out."

Zane called a cab to take Toni home. He saw her settled safely inside with regret—more regret than he usually felt at the end of an evening with a beautiful and enticing woman. Her mix of bold femininity and practical business sense surprised him. Mystified him. While this night hadn't ended as he'd planned, with Toni naked in his arms, there would be other nights for pleasure. He would see to it. Just like he now had to see to getting out the paper.

TONI WINCED AT THE bright morning sunlight pouring into her bedroom. Sleepy, attempting to hide despite the obviously late hour, she ducked her head under her pillow, but Bobby tugged the pillow away and squealed, "Oh, no, you don't."

It took a moment for coherent thoughts to run through her mind. Then last night came back. Striking up a conversation with Grey. Allowing her reckless streak a free rein. Dancing with Grey. Kissing Grey. Leaving Club Carnal. The photographers. The vandalism. She frowned. Grey apologetically sending her home in a cab and making no mention of their getting together again.

"Look!" Jude thrust a paper in her face.

Squinting, Toni peered at the rag without much interest in the headline, which read, Elvis Alive And Well In Key Largo. It was next to a picture of a two-headed whale that also failed to gain her attention.

Mickey shoved a cup of coffee into Toni's hand. "Give her a moment to wake up."

"You did it!" Bobby bounced on the bed, almost spilling Toni's coffee. "The way you throw yourself into every project, I had no doubt you'd succeed. You're right there with Grey Masterson on page seven."

Toni gulped her coffee, desperate for a caffeine jolt. But what perked her up was the sight of her and Grey's handsome face in full color, Club Carnal's neon sign clear in the background, while up close and personal, Grey's arm was wrapped around her shoulder. In the picture, her face was in profile, but clear enough for anyone who knew her to identify her.

Bobby pointed to the caption with the tip of a pink nail. "Grey Masterson parties at Club Carnal with Toni Maxwell, a lady with a Feminine Touch."

"It's perfect," Jude crowed. "Senator Birdstrum has already left two messages on the answering machine. He's got to ask for his ring back now. I didn't want to wake you earlier but I think you'd better take his next call."

Her stomach unsettled, Toni sipped her coffee and stared at the picture. She and Grey both looked startled, but happy. The free advertisement of Grey's hot expression as he stared at her in that dress should start a new fashion craze. Just looking at that picture of him caused butterflies to swarm in her tummy. It had been so long since she'd been interested in a man that she'd forgotten how gratifying it could be.

She missed the on-the-edge, fly-by-the-seat-of-her-pants feeling of not knowing what would come next. She believed deeply that relationships shouldn't stand still or they would stagnate. Although she and Grey were not yet a couple, they could be. Especially since their evening had gone so well.

Satisfaction that the reporter had gone to the trouble to find out her name zinged through her, and the publicity about Feminine Touch would be terrific for business. Her plan appeared to have worked, but she felt off balance, slightly disappointed that Grey hadn't called. However, it was only ten o'clock, and he might not have her phone number, although she imagined a resourceful newspaperman like him could get it.

After meeting Grey last night, after enjoying his male magnetism and recognizing their mutual attraction, her feelings for him had become much more personal. She should have been satisfied that she'd gotten exactly what she wanted. Technically, that part of her plan had succeeded, but she didn't feel as if her task was done. She wanted more. More time with Grey.

But he hadn't called and she made excuses for him. *He worked half the night. He's probably still asleep.* And she'd gone to bed hours before him and she'd just awakened. There was no reason for disappointment. Where was all her confidence from the night before?

Last night had been fun. Although she had acted so much bolder than her normal self, there was a part of her that had enjoyed her uninhibited behavior. If their evening hadn't been interrupted, she wasn't sure that she wouldn't have ended up in Grey's bed.

The portable phone in Mickey's apron pocket rang. Toni's hopes rose that Grey might be the caller. Mickey plucked the phone out and checked the caller ID. "It's the senator."

Resigned, Toni held out her hand for the phone, knowing that if she put off the unpleasant call with Senator Birdstrum, it would weigh on her all day. "Hello?"

She tried to shoo her sisters out of her room, but without success. Clearly, they intended to keep prying into her life.

And then the senator distracted her from all thoughts of privacy.

"Toni, darling."

Darling?

She'd expected hurt, withdrawal, maybe an accusation—not an endearment. Maybe he hadn't seen the picture and was calling about another matter. "Senator?"

"I don't want you to be upset."

Why would she be upset? "I'm not."

"I'm a man of the world. I understand how these things happen. Don't even worry your little head about that picture or how it looks."

What?

Normally, she would have bristled at his condescending tone, but she was simply too flabbergasted to react to being patronized. She needed to set him straight. Immediately. Or all her planning would have been for nothing. "You—"

"I know just what happened," he interrupted kindly. "No doubt, you and Grey Masterson left the club at the same time, and when those photographers accosted you, Mr. Masterson simply tried to protect you. I would have done the same thing for a pretty lady in distress."

"I wasn't in distress. Look—"

"I'm sorry I wasn't there to protect you from those paparazzi vultures. I'll have to call Mr. Masterson later to thank him personally."

"But—"

"I've got to go."

"Wait—"

"Sorry, darling. They need me for a vote."

The phone went dead. Sheesh! The senator hadn't allowed her to get in a word of explanation and her frustration mounted. Had all her scheming last night been for nothing?

Her sisters must have read a look of distress on her face because Jude put an arm over her shoulder, Bobby patted her hand and Mickey sighed. ''Tell us.''

''Did he see the picture?''

''Is he mad?''

''Did he ask for his ring back?''

''No, no and no. He forgives me.'' Toni threw a hand up in the air in disgust. ''He thinks the entire incident was a mistake.''

''So much for creating a sex scandal,'' Mickey said.

Bobby frowned. ''We'll just have to think of another way to convince him he doesn't want her.''

''How?'' Toni looked at her sisters. ''I'm sending that ring back today, but I suspect he'll convince himself that it's the ring I don't like, not him.'' Of the four of them, Toni was the one who always threw herself wholeheartedly into each project, and she expected to succeed. Usually hard work and persistence were enough to achieve her goals. Obviously, this time, more was required. Yet she fully intended to achieve her goal. And with her sisters' help, she was sure they would come up with a solution.

Bobby smoothed her sheet. ''You could eat like crazy and make yourself fat. A man like the senator, so conscience of image, would be embarrassed to be seen with an overweight woman.'' Bobby must have seen their looks of doubt. ''He never asked *me* out,'' she added. Again Toni wondered about Bobby's seeming infatuation with the senator, which her sister continued to deny.

''He never asked Jude out either,'' Toni told Bobby gently. While Bobby had lost all those pounds, her psyche still remained sensitive to the prejudices against overweight people.

Mickey absently tapped her foot against the bed frame and drew their attention. "It's unhealthy to put on weight that fast, you know that. Besides, gaining weight to repel a man is no healthier than losing weight to catch one."

Jude sighed. "You could develop, on purpose, a case of bromidrosis."

"Bromidrosis?" Bobby asked.

"It's stink foot." Toni rolled her eyes at the ceiling. "Thanks, but no thanks."

Jude took a seat at the foot of the bed, unwilling to give up her idea easily. "All you'd have to do is wear the same sneakers without any socks for a week. My ex-boyfriend had the stink down to a science."

"Think again." Toni appreciated the help, she did, but going around with stink foot was no solution. However, she didn't want to rein in their enthusiasm. Maybe they'd come up with an outrageous plan that could work.

Bobby grinned impishly. "What about another date with the eminently handsome and very charming Grey Masterson?"

"She's been there, done that," Jude argued. "Besides, Grey Masterson might not be so amenable to being stalked again."

Toni recalled dancing in bubbles and the delicious heat in Grey's eyes. "Grey Masterson will cooperate." She liked this idea already.

Mickey's practical eyebrows rose with skepticism. "Toni, are you willing to go further? No holds barred?"

"What do you mean?" Jude asked.

"She means," Toni answered with a blend of rising excitement and heart-pummeling trepidation, "am I willing to create a *real* scandal?"

ZANE ARRIVED AT Muriel's on Chartres Street in the French Quarter with barely a minute to spare to make the 7:00 p.m. appointment. After working half the night, grabbing two hours of sleep and a shower, he'd been back at the office by seven. The paper had successfully gone out in a fleet of rental cars, and mechanics had worked through the day to drain the fuel tanks and to repair the damaged trucks. Zane had hired new guards to prevent a repetition of last night's vandalism, but he kept wondering what he might have forgotten or left vulnerable to sabotage.

All during his busy day, memories of his evening with Toni Maxwell had stayed with him, but prevented him from phoning her. She could very well be his saboteur, so he wanted every security precaution in place before inviting her back into his life—which he most definitely intended to do. The puzzle she represented bedeviled him to the point that even a short two hours of sleep had been filled with dreams of her smiling at him. Whether she'd been laughing with him or at him, he'd never determined.

While Muriel's served terrific food in an elegant atmosphere that did New Orleans proud, Zane would have much preferred to be elsewhere. He tugged at the tie at his neck, wanting to beg out of this dinner with the mayor and chief of police, but if he insulted Grey's prominent friends, his brother wouldn't forgive him. His own newspaper had written articles about tonight's event, where New Orleans's business leaders would discuss options for bidding for the summer Olympic Games, so he couldn't claim he'd forgotten.

Just as he walked through the front door, Toni strode around the corner toward him. Dressed for dinner in a sleek black dress, a silk scarf sparkling with glass beads and high spiked heels, she spoke softly. "Hi, Grey."

He supposed he shouldn't have been surprised that she was stalking him again, but he was. And he was pleased. "Let me guess. You were waiting for me?"

"Not for very long." She slipped her arm through his, and he noted that she also had silver glitter in her hair and dusted over her shoulders. "You're right on time."

Over the years he'd had a few persistent women hound him with phone calls. But never one who'd inserted herself into his life with such bravura as his present dinner companion had. "How did you know—"

"I read your newspaper."

"Suppose I'd brought a date?"

"You didn't." As the maître d' came up to seat them, she winked at him and lowered her tone to a provocative murmur. "I thought we could take up where we left off last night."

Oh, she did, did she? Did she intend to get personal? While that notion both intrigued him and filled him with anticipation, he had to wonder whether she intended to prevent him from returning to the paper after dinner, so her partner could wreak havoc on the business again. If this was her scheme, the plans would fail. He'd made more than adequate preparation for such an eventuality.

So he had no qualms about whispering into her ear, "What exactly do you have in mind?"

She grinned. "A few kisses."

Kisses? Zane wondered where those kisses might lead, but didn't have the opportunity to ask her more, since they'd reached their table.

The meal was delicious but boring, so after dessert, they escaped the dinner party as quickly as was polite. Zane brought her upstairs for an after-dinner cocktail in the Seance Lounge. With its bordello-red velvet decor, soft lighting, plush sofa and stone fireplace, the bar perfectly mirrored his thoughts of seduction.

Sitting on a bar stool, crossing one shapely leg over the other, Toni cocked her head to one side and considered him. "You look exhausted."

"I didn't sleep much last night," he admitted, determined to let her lead the conversation, curious to see where she would go.

"I'm sorry." She started to slip off her stool. "Perhaps we should talk another time."

If she thought he could go to sleep after she'd shown up looking hot enough to draw looks from every man over the age of consent, he would have to be a man with no passion, no curiosity. He'd have to be half dead. Because if she had calculated her actions to make him burn with curiosity, she'd succeeded.

And he still didn't know why the hell she was here.

While she really did seem concerned about his lack of sleep, he could tell she had something weighty on her mind by the way she hesitated, almost waiting for him to keep her from leaving. He'd play along. "I'm fine."

She edged back onto the stool and played with the rim of her glass with a fingertip. "Today was hectic in my shop. That picture in the paper sold lots of dresses."

Her sudden change of topic caused a light to go on

in his mind. She wanted to be seen with him for the publicity. Publicity brought customers into her boutique. Although slightly disappointed at such a mundane reason, he wanted her to be innocent of the problems at the paper. Finally, he had some clue to why she'd been stalking his brother. After Lane Morrow's book, Grey was enduring his fifteen minutes of fame—Toni Maxwell wanted to share that fame to garner business for her store.

"So hanging out with me is good for business?"

Her eyes flickered with an emotion he couldn't read. Surprise? Sorrow? Hesitation? He had the feeling that the bold seductive maneuvers weren't the norm for her. Or was she simply hiding another damn secret?

"I need publicity," she admitted, dipping one fingertip into her glass then touching it to her tongue in a sexy gesture that he refused to allow to distract him from concentrating on her words. "The more publicity, the better. And creating a scandal will create lots of publicity."

"Let me get this straight. You *want* to create a scandal?"

"Yes."

"What kind of scandal?"

"The sexual kind. And I don't see why those sleazy tabloids should make all the money off of us."

If he hadn't had only one drink, he could have blamed his lack of comprehension on the alcohol. But he was sober and didn't have an excuse. If she didn't want the tabloids to print her sexual scandal, then was she insinuating that he print their story? She couldn't be proposing what he thought she was. "What are you saying? That you want me to cover our sex scandal in the *Louisiana Daily Herald?*"

She took a deep breath and let it out slowly. "It might raise circulation."

Zane bit back a chuckle at her outrageous idea. Yet...increasing circulation was just what the paper needed right now. If she was right, and profits increased, no one would have to be fired, a task he knew Grey had been putting off.

She cocked her head, then licked her bottom lip, possibly from nerves, but she seemed very sure of herself. The contrast kept him intrigued, yet he also found the dichotomy in her behavior confusing.

"Do we have a deal?" she asked, her tone brazen, her expression just a bit hesitant.

"Let's be very clear here. You want us to create a sex scandal and for me to write about it in the paper?"

"Yes."

"You realize that creating a scandal in a city as decadent as New Orleans requires extra shockability to work on the public?"

"I do."

"You're prepared to go to the extreme?"

"I am."

A good thing he and Grey had switched places. He couldn't imagine his conservative twin accepting her bargain, let alone keeping his cool when such an attractive woman made the offer. On the other hand, Zane planned to enjoy himself fully. Of course, she'd believe she would be having sex with Grey, and Zane would be writing up their affair as if he were Grey. It was completely insane, but Zane would agree to her scheme for his own reasons. Staying close to her would allow him to ascertain if she was his saboteur—and he could enjoy himself at the same time.

''Exactly how far are you prepared to go?'' he asked, his mouth dry, his voice even.

''That depends on you,'' she countered, her grin tantalizing. ''And how innovative you can be.''

5

ALTHOUGH TONI HAD SOUGHT to add passion to her life, she could barely believe she was this bold woman issuing challenging words like some kind of accomplished seductress. While she certainly was no blushing virgin, her sexual experiences had always been what she thought of as average. The location had usually been a bed, the positions had been limited to a few favorites, and the number of partners hadn't been excessive. Nothing too unusual.

Her quest for a relationship with Grey Masterson had freed her of her ordinary inhibitions. In her business life, she'd always gone for risks. She could have taken a safe job with another designer and assured herself of a weekly paycheck, but instead she'd sunk every penny into opening up Feminine Touch and had existed on a shoestring for six nail-biting months. Making independent and risky decisions, knowing she was solely responsible for whether she succeeded or failed, had suited her. The challenging experience had been one of the most exhilarating in her life.

However, her social existence had become way too conservative. Perhaps she'd unconsciously figured that one major risk at a time was all the challenge she could bear. But now that her business talents were gaining attention, now that her designs were considered trendy, and the boutique was showing a steadily increasing profit, she was ready to take on the ultimate risk in her personal life. The risk of throwing caution to fate, the risk of throwing herself at sexy Grey Masterson.

Creating a scandal may have begun as a crazy idea to protect her father from the wrath of a jilted senator, but there were other advantages to her scheme. The simmering chemistry between Grey and herself had her eager to experiment. No matter how much she loved her father, no matter how much she didn't want to hurt him or Bobby, who may or may not be interested in the senator herself, Toni would never take this next step unless *she* wanted Grey.

Now, her desire had taken on a dimension all its own. She found herself holding her breath, waiting to see what he would do next. Though she'd read Lane Morrow's book, she'd never expected to like Grey as much as did, or want him as much as she did. And while *Cosmopolitan* didn't suggest stalking as one of the ten top ways to meet a man, Toni would be a fool to back out now. Not when he looked good enough to eat for dessert. Not when the mere heat in his blue eyes, fringed with dark lashes, shot straight to her core. Not when she'd never ached so much for a man's kiss as she did for his.

He cupped the back of her neck with a warm, firm touch that took control of her. "I can be very innovative."

"I'm counting on it," she murmured, anticipating his lips touching hers. Her mouth ready, her body arching, she leaned toward him.

Over her head, Grey locked eyes with the bartender and tipped his head toward the door. She heard the server head through the arched doorway, leaving them to their privacy. They currently had the semiprivate room to themselves, and while she was fully aware that anyone could walk in at any time, the hour was late. Although an interruption was unlikely, it was possible.

Grey dipped his head until his lips moved to within a whisper of hers. ''You think kissing in a public place is scandalous?''

''That would depend on the kiss.''

Ever so slowly, his gaze riveted on hers, he lowered his mouth. She clenched her hands around his neck, tugging him closer. Close enough to feel the heat radiating from him. Close enough to see the pulse in his neck throb. Close enough to hear his breath skip. And while his tongue swept her into what felt like a riptide of sensation, his hand drifted from her neck, divesting her of her scarf, letting the silk and beads clatter to the floor. With her bare shoulders exposed, he peeled down the zipper at the back of her dress. In no rush, he worked slowly, giving her time to pull away from his mouth or to object to unzipping.

The cool air on the bared skin of her back, tempered by the heat of his fingers, shocked her almost as much as the thought of disrobing in a public place. And while his devastating kiss had her trembling for much more, she still weighed the risk of discovery. She doubted they'd be arrested. Worst-case scenario would be major embarrassment, which she could handle, if necessary.

With her mind made up to let the storm of his passion float her away on whatever course he chose, she gave herself up to enjoying the marvelous sensations rippling through her, the warmth of his hands on her shoulders stoking a matching need in her to remove his clothes.

She raised her fingers to loosen his tie, but the straps of her dress tangled around her wrists, trapping her hands at her sides. She shook an arm to free herself, and he pulled back his mouth enough to whisper, "Don't move. I want to thoroughly enjoy this moment."

He dropped his gaze to her bared breasts and her nipples immediately pebbled.

She swallowed hard. She was sitting half-naked in a bar, before a man who seemed totally in control of himself, while she felt as though she was going to come apart at loosened seams if he didn't touch her. Now.

All he seemed to want to do was look. She tried to keep petulance from her tone. "I can't just sit here while you look at me."

"Why not?" His tone, husky but amused, poured through her like fine brandy, intoxicating her senses, firing her blood. "Looking at you gives me pleasure. And you do want to give me pleasure, don't you?"

"Yes." She'd never wanted a man so badly that her knees quivered. But she didn't want him to know that she was already weak when he'd merely kissed her.

"If you'd like us both to enjoy a scandalous experience, you'll have to be patient," he warned, his eyes blazing with heat. "Can you be patient?"

She gritted her teeth as his gaze roved over her exposed curves. She didn't mind him looking, or enjoying her body, but, damn it, what was he waiting for?

Wet heat had dampened her panties, and she ached for him to touch her. And while she'd accepted the consequences of being caught in public, fast, hard sex would lower the risk. Obviously, Grey didn't mind taking risks, but he wasn't the one standing naked. Exposed. Vulnerable.

"Can you be patient?" he repeated.

"Grey, if you don't do something, I'm going to—"

"I *am* doing something. I'm looking at the most beautiful woman I've seen in a long time. Desire makes your gray eyes darken. Your lips are full from my kisses and—"

"Stop teasing me."

"Why?"

"Because I need more than your gaze on my body."

"You aren't aroused by a compliment?"

She spoke through jaws clenched with frustration. "I need more."

He licked the tip of his finger, slowly wetting the skin as he sucked on the tip, taunting her as he silently promised a reward if she could summon up additional patience. She held her breath. Finally, he touched the tip of her nipple.

At the dampness, combined with the cool air and the rasp of his finger which drew her focus, she gasped. Her breasts swelled achingly. How had he made her so sensitive to his slightest caress? So eager to go further, do more, be more than ever before? As though a wildness inside raged to let loose, she urged him on.

"I need more," she demanded again, slightly breathless.

His finger transferred to her other breast. "Look at me."

Oh God! She tilted her head, let him see her need, the gesture more exhilarating and more intimate than any she'd yet experienced with this man. A man she barely knew.

His cheeks chiseled with determination, his mouth firm with resolve, he demanded, "Are you aroused?"

"You need to ask?"

"How long can you hold back?"

His question shocked her. She was ready. Ready to

climax. First, he'd wanted to look at her, now he wanted to talk. Couldn't he just get on with seducing her? Why did he have to make her wait? "What's the point?"

"Ah." He smiled then, a predatory grin that told her she was way out of her league. She had no idea where he was taking her. No idea what he was thinking. In fact, she wasn't sure what *she* was thinking. She only knew that she'd never felt so sure that she could climax with just one tiny caress in the right place—a place Grey seemed in no rush to explore.

Instead he seemed intent in keeping her on this nerve-wracking edge of heat, where she could barely think, or breathe, or function. And the passion roaring through her frightened her almost as much as it exhilarated her. He seemed to have stripped away any thought of responsibility, of doing the right thing. And he'd left her with need. A need to have him kiss her, touch her, stroke her. Her every thought of *him.*

And then like a lightning bolt striking and searing, she understood the answer to her own question. Orgasm and release would be wonderful. The final destination mattered, but the journey could be just as important.

Grey wanted to focus on the journey.

With every other man, she'd rushed through each step of that first flush of romance and passion, anxious to see if that man was *the right one.* And when she'd discovered her other men hadn't been special enough, or a good enough match, she'd moved on. Grey wasn't about to let that happen. He was in no rush to reach the end of their journey together, instead he wanted to enjoy each kiss, each caress, each moment along the way.

His perceptiveness struck a chord in her, a response that rang true. She'd been reckless and uninhibited before, but she'd never given passion free rein to completely overrule her reliable and conscientious side. Understanding now caused her to square her shoulders and lift her chin in preparation to answer him. She sensed tonight was a test. A test she was determined to ace. The opportunity to explore a sexual relationship with Grey was one that might change her irrevocably, one that she instinctively understood would challenge her and perhaps push her out of her comfort zone, but one she must take—for herself.

"We'll do this your way," she agreed, her heart skipping as if she'd just agreed to step on a high wire with no safety net below. "I'll learn to be patient."

"Good." His hands slipped under her skirt and removed her panties. He thrust them into his pocket, and she sensed he wouldn't be returning them. Just the thought that he wanted an intimate article of her clothing caused her to part her legs as wide as her skirt allowed.

His strong fingers skimming her thighs had left her knees trembling and the rest of her eager for more of his touch. He was testing her again, testing her determination and patience. While she tried to tell herself her reaction was simply due to the lack of lovemaking in her life—she knew better. Being with Grey was special because he drew out each little nuance and carefully provoked her reactions to him.

"You know what I'd like to do?" he asked.

"What?"

"Skim my fingers up along the inside of your thighs and feel your heat."

"Are you waiting for a written invitation?" she

countered, somewhat shocked by her behavior and realizing that acquiring patience would take a diligent effort that might tax her to the limit. Yet, she sensed the rewards would prove spectacular, even if allowing him to take charge left her feeling more vulnerable than she'd ever felt before.

He checked his watch. "This place is closing in five minutes, so we're both going to wait."

What? "Exactly how long are we going to wait?"

"We'll make love soon. I promise."

Disappointment, confusion and hurt flashed through her. And anger that he would leave her unsatisfied. The restaurant might be closing, but he could take her home or bring her to a hotel—but no. He intended to leave her clinging to hope. She hadn't missed that he hadn't given her a specific day or time. She yanked up her dress and struggled with the zipper.

Gently, he turned her around, his fingers warm and gentle on her shoulders, then he zipped up her dress. "Trust me. I'm worth the wait."

"You damn well better be." She tamped down her desire. She would not reveal to him her ragged emotions, so confused, so intense, she couldn't sort them out.

But he knew. She could see it in the banked heat of his eyes when he kissed her. Only for a moment did she accept his soothing lips. Placing her palms on his chest, she shoved him back and held out her hand. "I want my panties."

"No."

No? "What, you need a trophy?" she snapped at him, annoyed she'd been right when she'd guessed he'd keep them, and now truly furious, her emotions swinging wildly to and fro as she dealt with both her vulnerability and her need to continue. She'd wanted so much more, more of his kisses, more of his touch, and dealing with the lack of an orgasm and a sense of completion had thrown her more than she wanted to admit to herself.

He shook his head. "I want you to think about me with every step you take."

"Bastard."

He grinned. "Don't put on another pair."

Now he was telling her how to dress? "Arrogant bastard."

His grin widened. "Sleep naked tonight and don't satisfy yourself."

"Go to hell." If Grey was determined to push her further than she'd believed she had the ability to cope with, he'd have to deal with her fury. That she hadn't run out of here screaming proved to her that she was either an idiot or stronger than she'd known. And his taking her to the edge and back had opened up a floodgate of emotions.

He spoke in a conversational tone with a hint of steel beneath. "I want you to think about me having free access to touching you. Whenever we meet again."

God. "You want me to stay aroused and wait for you? Are you nuts? Why should I do that? How do I know we'll even see one another again or that next time you won't disappoint me again?"

"Because, as I think about you, I'll be just as aroused and just as uncomfortable. And when we finally come together, it'll be indescribable."

His words promised, persuaded and provoked. She didn't know whether to laugh or cry. Kiss him or kill him. But something had happened to her tonight. She wanted to explore her sexuality, see where he would take her. She had to take this journey. And after he'd admitted he wanted her as badly as she wanted him, her anger dissipated, leaving just the aftereffects of what he'd done to her—a pounding pulse, an accelerated heartbeat and a tension that gave her courage.

"Okay." She agreed to his terms, remembering Lane Morrow's book and her claim that he'd taken her places she'd never been. Shown her sights she'd never seen. And even knowing that going along with him might be the most difficult experience of Toni's life, she would never forgive herself if she walked away now.

"You know what I need to do tonight?" he whispered in her ear as they left the restaurant.

"What?" She expected him to tease her with more talk of sex, perhaps tell her how he intended to get ready for their next date.

"I've got to write a few words about our evening together for tomorrow's morning edition of the *Louisiana Daily Herald* to create your scandal. It might be easier to write if I knew *why* you wanted a sex scandal."

Toni grinned. "No one ever said life was easy."

ZANE TOOK TONI BACK TO the office with him, hoping she would fuel his creativity. The newspaper remained open twenty-four hours a day, seven days a week, and at this time of night, the building was mostly staffed with production people. Only a few reporters remained on shift.

Zane escorted Toni up to the newly hired watchman who eyed her long legs with appreciation, but remained professional and asked them for identification and for Toni to sign in as a guest. Zane was gratified to see that his security detail followed the protocols he'd established, but he also realized that bringing Toni to the newspaper premises would make a statement to the employees that the boss had a new lady. She looked slightly sleepy-eyed, but sexy as all get-out in her little black dress and snappy heels. Gossip would fly and add fodder to the story he was about to write.

Zane did nothing to hide his admiration of Toni. He hoped her lipstick had smudged on his neck. He hoped as they strolled through the building in their evening attire that employees would guess what they had been doing. Tomorrow, when the paper hit the streets, everyone would know.

However, he'd heard Grey often talk about the business and knew that just because a story made it to print, the public didn't always take it as truth. With the kind of scandal he intended to build, they needed to be seen together and he hoped the sparks between them would be as apparent to others as they were to him.

He didn't exactly know how or when, but he felt a connection with Toni Maxwell, businesswoman, femme fatale, stalker. She fascinated and intrigued him. And he found himself relishing his switch with Grey more than he'd ever imagined, mostly due to Toni's company. But as much as Zane would like to give her all the credit, he couldn't.

He'd actually liked solving the multitude of problems that had cropped up during his short time here. His enjoyment of the challenge to pull this business out of the red and into the black was starting to make him wonder if he still wanted a life of leisure. But how long before Zane would tire of running this business? How long before he would miss breakfast at noon, elegant dinners at midnight and hanging with his jet-set friends?

With the newspaper filling every minute of his days, and Toni to keep him company at night, he might be content for a while. And a while was longer than usual. So he would take this opportunity and see where it led—especially if it took him into Toni's arms and her bed.

After taking the elevator to the top floor where Grey's office dominated half the penthouse administrative suite, they entered the outer sanctum where the managing editor, Stephen Robbards, diligently worked through stacks of paperwork.

"Stephen." Zane knocked, then entered the managing editor's office. Six foot five inches, rail thin and with drooping brown eyes bleary from reading too much copy, Stephen peered at Zane, then Toni, with puzzlement. Zane put an arm around Toni's waist and drew her against his side, leaving no doubt of their relationship. "I'd like to introduce you to Toni Maxwell. Save me a column on page one in tomorrow's edition. I'm going to write a story about us."

Stephen grinned and offered Toni a large hand to shake. "Pleased to meet you, ma'am." Then he turned to Zane. "You're kidding, right?"

"Wrong."

"But we put the paper to bed in less than an hour."

"Then I'd better get cracking. Wouldn't want to miss the deadline," Zane spoke lightly, hoping the managing editor wouldn't suddenly drop dead of a heart attack. Stephen appeared about to choke on his former grin. His face suffused with color. He rose to his feet, confusion making him stumble with clumsiness.

Zane quickly guided Toni into a turnaround and started to ease her through the door.

''Wait.'' Stephen frowned at them. From one of the more conservative old money Louisiana families, he was Grey's right-hand man, running the entire operation during the night hours and leaving only after Grey's arrival in the morning. While Zane was certain Stephen didn't have a clue that his boss had switched places with his twin, the man was looking at Zane as if he had suddenly sprouted three heads. To his credit, his tone remained polite. ''Would you like me to send in a reporter to help?''

''No, thanks.'' Zane continued walking, expecting to leave a sputtering Stephen behind.

However, the man had more presumptuousness than Zane had given him credit for, following them out the door and into the hallway. ''Sir, may I ask the story's subject matter?''

''Sure,'' Zane kept his feet moving. ''I'm going to write about New Orleans's hottest sex scandal.''

''What sex scandal?'' When Zane didn't reply, Stephen didn't give up, dogging their footsteps. ''Perhaps you should consult with our attorney. We don't want to open ourselves to a lawsuit.''

''Not a problem,'' Zane countered.

''Sir, think of the liability. Do you have two reliable witnesses willing to confirm the details?''

Zane winked at Toni, who had tried and failed to bite back a grin. ''That's why I brought Ms. Maxwell with me. She'll give me details from the woman's perspective.''

''I will?'' Toni looked up at him, mischief gleaming in her eyes.

Stephen looked like a man who'd just eaten a sour

pickle, and couldn't swallow or find a place to spit. "I really don't think that this is a good—"

"A sex scandal will sell newspapers," Zane told him.

"This paper has always been—"

"Too conservative," Zane argued.

"But without quality reporting, you'll drag this paper's reputation through the dirt. Your grandfather—"

"Liked to turn a profit. Stephen, if we don't raise our circulation, there will be no paper. And no jobs."

Zane had reached Grey's office and let the door slide shut behind him and Toni, leaving Stephen to sputter in the hallway. He couldn't worry about the *Herald*'s reputation—not since he'd reviewed the balance sheets. Something had to be done. And quickly.

Tonight he would put his journalism degree to use for the first time since he'd graduated college. While Toni used the rest room, Zane took a few minutes to call Grey and coax his consent for Zane to do whatever he wished with the paper. Grey, surprisingly, said he just couldn't think about business right now and that Zane had free rein to do what he liked.

Zane wondered if Grey would still feel that way after reading the story about himself on page one. But with a midnight deadline looming, Zane had to get moving. With a burst of inspiration, he decided to create his own column and byline called "Hot Scoops." Sitting in front of the computer, he cracked his rusty knuckles and began to type.

He described Grey's fascination with a certain lady who went by the initials T.M., about how the sounds and the sights and the tastes of New Orleans had led him into a homegrown romance with one of the city's most elegant career women. He wrote about how sexy he found matching wits with her. He described the outfit she'd worn to Club Carnal and the dress she'd worn to the restaurant in detail, down to the built-in bra and exactly how fine she looked to him. He reconstructed and summarized their conversation, and their hot kiss in the red velvet room, hinted how they'd gotten carried away, that one of them had partially disrobed. And as he wrote, he got turned on all over again, remembering her taste, her soft skin and her trembling response to him.

He ended the column with the comment that Grey Masterson had certainly moved on from Lane Morrow to someone much more intriguing. And that readers could expect the next installment in two more days, after the couple had a chance to become much better acquainted, especially since the lady had promised not to wear panties until they met again.

He read over his story, did a word count and spell check, then carefully perused for typographical errors and punctuation mistakes, already knowing that no matter how perfect his grammar, the staid newspaper would receive a slew of complaints. At least he had no board of directors to please. With his and Grey's parents retired and on a semipermanent tour of the world, Zane had no one to please but himself.

He hit the print button, intending to read his work aloud one more time before shooting it down to production. He'd been so engrossed in capturing on paper the romantic mood of the evening, he'd forgotten the woman who'd made the column possible.

Toni. Where was she?

He snagged the printed column from the printer and checked his watch with a frown. Toni had abandoned him for the rest room, almost forty minutes ago.

He strode out of his office to find her sitting at his secretary's desk, her head pillowed on her arms, sound asleep. He imagined that she'd peeked into his office, found him typing madly and hadn't wanted to disturb him. Touched by her consideration, he vowed to make it up to her.

But, first, he needed an eye-catching picture for "Hot Scoops." Perhaps a gown, or maybe a pair of shoes.

Recalling that he'd read a story the paper had once done on Toni's boutique, Zane checked through the files and found a sensational image of a flirty blue dress designed by Toni. Carefully, he centered the picture and placed a caption at the bottom. Perfect. The image depicted class, and the story remained edgy. He expected circulation to go up. Hoped Toni would be pleased. And he muffled a chuckle as he tried not to think about his conservative twin's reaction to reading about his newest lover.

With a few added keystrokes, Zane bypassed the proofreader and sent the picture and story straight to production. His work for the day finished, Zane's attention focused on the sleeping woman in the next room and he decided he wasn't taking her home. Tomorrow was Sunday, and her store would be closed.

He picked up the phone and began to make arrangements. The best part about wealth was that, at any time of the day or night, money could buy luxury and convenience. Zane asked Grey's butler to pack two travel bags, one for him and another for the lady. In addition, Zane called a friend who never slept until dawn and asked him to deliver a very special package of goodies from his specialty shop to the *Herald*'s rooftop.

Zane and Grey both had their helicopter pilot's license and Grey's chopper was on the roof. Zane remembered Grey's island, bequeathed to him by their *grand-mère,* the same great-grandmother who had left Zane the Garden District home he now leased to Reina Price. Neither one of the brothers visited the private island often, but a live-in cook and handyman looked after the beach house and stables in case of last-minute jaunts. Zane couldn't think of a better locale than the Roquellaire island for the scandalous activities he had in mind.

If Toni had other plans for tomorrow, she'd just have to cancel them.

6

HALF AWAKE, TONI LIFTED her head from the desk where she'd fallen asleep waiting for Grey to finish typing their story. No matter what else happened between them, she would always treasure the memory of him pounding his keyboard with such ferocity, eyebrows drawn together in concentration, a sexy smile playing on his lips. Blue light had shined on his glossy dark hair and had cast shadows on sharp, intense cheekbones, as he'd leaned aggressively forward, that complex smile haunting his face.

Apparently, he'd enjoyed their evening as much as she had. She could have called a cab and gone home, but she'd been reluctant to part without saying goodbye, had been reluctant to leave him, period, and no way could she bring herself to interrupt him.

Toni might not know a thing about the newspaper business, but she understood the fragile process of creativity. When she penciled her designs, the uninterrupted flow came from a place that she couldn't tap on demand. Her ideas came in spurts. Bright, hard and fast. And she'd draw furiously, one idea prodding the next. Stopping would not only break the flow, she could lose that particular idea forever. So she'd napped, unwilling to interfere with his flow of words. And now he stood over her in his secretary's office with that mixture of intensity and amusement that seemed uniquely his.

"All done?" she asked. Stretching, she glanced up to find Grey's expression tender, a hint of devilry in his eyes. Her first stretch had been to ease her aching bones, the second was pure female ego as she arched her back and raised her arms above her head, drawing attention to her chest. She liked watching his gaze slide downward from her face, liked that he didn't even attempt to hide his appreciation of her body.

Before they'd met, she'd pegged Grey for a conservative businessman whose private desires had been outed by Lane Morrow's book. And when she'd stalked him and he'd resisted, her original idea about him had been confirmed. Yet, sometime between her embarrassing him in her gorilla suit and his appearing at Club Carnal, his personality had done a one-eighty. This Grey wasn't just relaxed about his sexuality, he embraced it.

"The article is finished, but, lady, I'm not done with you." His voice, low and deep, shimmied over her with serene composure and shot a wake-up call to her brain. She'd known Grey Masterson was powerful, influential, but she hadn't anticipated that she'd find his unique intensity so seductive. She sensed from the tightness in her throat to the curling in her toes that if she intended to back out of their bargain, now was the time.

Clearly, he was up to something. She could read it in his expression as he watched her like a hungry jungle cat about to pounce on tasty prey.

Tossing her hair over her shoulder, she stood, retrieved her beaded scarf and stretched again. "That's why I waited right here. I'm not done with you, either.''

''Good. Let's go.'' He slipped his arm through hers, the gesture so gentle and civilized that she actually felt safe—until he pressed the up button of the elevator.

Grey's office was on the top floor. She turned to him in confusion. ''Where—''

''You'll see.''

The elevator opened onto the building's flat rooftop. Leaving the air-conditioning behind, the warm night air wrapped around them while moonlight lit their way. A helicopter sat on its pad, the baggage compartment open while a man in a uniform stowed luggage.

Did Grey intend to spirit her away? A shiver of pleasure shot through her. While she'd slept, Grey hadn't just written his article, he'd made plans…that included her. Yet back in the private room at the restaurant, he'd led her to believe that they wouldn't be seeing one another for a while. He'd specifically requested that she sleep naked, that he intended for her to stay aroused until they met again.

She spun to face him, her hands fisting on her hips. ''I thought we were going to delay being together.''

''*I* couldn't wait,'' he admitted with a sheepish grin that charmed her. ''Besides, tomorrow is Sunday and your boutique's closed. I thought I'd fly you away for what's left of the weekend.''

Without asking? Obviously, he didn't want to wait much longer to make love. She didn't know whether to be flattered, annoyed or impressed. However, she did feel a little thrilled that he'd gone to the trouble to make such decadent plans. For a supposedly conservative man, he seemed to enjoy extravagant gestures.

He motioned to the two-seater red-and-white painted

helicopter with the newspaper's logo on the tail. The craft looked fragile, the bubble Plexiglas front little protection from the elements, but she'd never flown in one and the notion excited her.

"You're a pilot?"

He nodded. "If there's anyone you need to call before we leave, you might want to do it now. Cell phones don't always work on the island."

"Island?" He didn't hear, or ignored, her question as he left her side to check over the helicopter.

She phoned home and left a message on the machine that her sisters shouldn't worry, telling them she'd be back no later than Monday morning. Realizing that Mickey would want more explanation, one Toni didn't want to give, she turned off the cell phone, justifying the action by reasoning that she didn't have a charger for her battery and needed to save it. Practical matters over and done, she joined Grey beside the helicopter.

Thinking that a quick trip home to pack might be in order, she tapped him on the shoulder. "I don't have a toothbrush."

"I have a spare."

She gestured to her cocktail dress. "But I don't even have a change of clothes."

"You won't need any," he said.

He must have read her expression of trepidation because he chuckled. "Don't worry. I've taken care of everything."

"But—"

"I consider it my personal mission to take care of you until Monday morning." He wagged his eyebrows in an exaggerated leer that almost made her chuckle. "You won't regret putting yourself into my hands."

From his tone, she couldn't miss the double entendre. And her mouth went dry. Without another word, she marched toward the helicopter's door. "Where should I sit?"

He strapped her into the passenger seat with efficient moves, then handed her a headset with a microphone, similar to the hands-free set she often used at work, but this one covered both ears instead of just one.

"Put this on," he instructed, suddenly all business. "It'll protect your ears. There's a radio in the headset that will enable us to talk to one another without noise interference from the engines."

She placed the headset over her ears. With efficient maneuvers that told her he'd done this many times before, he strapped himself in, then performed a thorough preflight check. After he turned on the engine, the overhead rotor slowly circled and gathered speed. The smooth liftoff reminded her of an amusement park ride. Once she got over the eerie feeling of sitting in a flying chair, a condition aggravated by the clear Plexiglas that began at the ceiling and curved to the floor, she took in the magnificent view of the city below.

Although she'd lived in New Orleans her entire life and knew the city and its surroundings reasonably well, she had difficulty getting her bearings. From overhead, the buildings, streets and parks looked different than from on the ground. The Mississippi River appeared like a dark snake winding and slicing through city lights.

Within minutes they left the shine of the city behind to fly over water which had to be Lake Borgne, the name misleading since this body of water connected to the Gulf of Mexico. She tested the microphone. "We're heading east?"

"Yes." His voice came through her headset as clearly as if he had spoken directly into her ear.

"Is your island part of Louisiana or Mississippi?"

He shrugged. "I have no idea."

"You don't know where we're going?"

He chuckled. "I could give you latitude and longitude. But I'd have to check our records to find out where we pay our real-estate taxes."

Must be nice to have so much property that one didn't know which state they were in. Grey's attitude toward piloting his helicopter to a private island was as casual as most men driving their car home. "You're taking me to the Masterson family vacation home?"

"Yes, though the island was left to me by my great-grandmother Roquellaire."

"What's it like?"

"Relaxing. Nice."

"It's kind of overwhelming the way you bog me down in details," she complained.

"You want details, I'll give you details." He glanced at her, his expression mischievous. "Louisiana and Mississippi's shoreline is like the edge of a fraying tapestry with thousands of barrier islands. Most are bird sanctuaries that house thousands of residents like gulls, terns, pelicans, plovers, wrens, rails and skimmers." Damn, she'd asked for details, not a lecture. Still, she couldn't help but be impressed by the scope of his knowledge as he continued. "In addition, there are millions of other birds which are part-time residents of the marshes—waterfowl from the north arrive in autumn, wading birds breed there in the spring. Huge herons and egrets and bitterns often fill the sky. And we have the tiny romantic hummingbirds and warblers and vireos, some flying from as far away as twenty-five hundred miles away.''

She thought of her sister who lobbied for every environmental cause that came down the pike. ''My sister Jude would be in heaven.'' However, she couldn't think about her sister for long. Grey had surprised her with his knowledge. Who would have figured the businessman for a bird enthusiast? Or a chopper pilot?

He seemed to know a lot about a great many things. She supposed that curiosity would be normal in a newspaperman, but the way he could concentrate intensely, then relax just as totally was a trait that kept taking her by surprise. Once away from his business, he didn't call in, didn't seem to worry or obsess the way she did about Feminine Touch. It was almost as if Grey the businessman was only one facet of his personality.

''The wild beauty of the island is as fascinating as the birds. My great-grandmother's family from Canada settled on the island and built the first structures. Storms occasionally wash away the house, but we always rebuild. And except for a few acres around the house and stables and a riding path, we've left the land natural. It's a natural salt dome.''

''What's a salt dome?'' she asked, content to listen to his husky voice in her ear, curious to see if his knowledge extended into yet another subject—geology.

''Our island, and three hundred others like it, are the product of salt beds, buried deep in the ground and formed over one hundred and fifty million years ago when the ancient sea became landlocked and then evaporated. Since the salt is light, it was gradually squeezed upward to form an island.''

She couldn't imagine much growing on top of salt. But she supposed the salt acted as a base, something she learned about on a trip her family had taken to Mt. Saint Helens. Ten years after a volcanic eruption, trees grew through the lava. And if birds lived on the island, the place couldn't be barren. But what interested her more than birds or geology was the way Grey spoke about the island. His knowledge gave away his fondness for the place.

"You took family vacations there?"

"Almost every summer. My brother and I ran wild, exploring and swimming and riding."

"There're just the two of you?" she asked. "You must be close."

"What about you?" he asked, avoiding her implied question. She thought it odd that this was the first time he'd mentioned his brother. But then they hadn't spent that much of their time together talking.

"Jude is the oldest, then Bobby, then me, and Mickey is the baby with a wise soul. After our folks moved to Baton Rouge two years ago, they sold the family home in the suburbs and my sisters and I bought the house in the French Quarter. We wanted to stay together."

He checked one of his scopes on the instrument panel and made a minor change in their direction. "Losing the home you grew up in isn't always easy."

"We all responded differently. Jude studies and promotes her causes. Bobby went on a diet and lost thirty pounds and Mickey is learning to be a chef. I buried myself in my designs and the store."

"Which is doing well and going to do better after my story in tomorrow's paper hits," he promised.

She felt guilty for misleading him. He'd been nothing but kind and decent to her. And before they made love, she wanted to tell him the truth. She figured now was as good a time as any to come clean. ''My boutique has nothing to do with…us.''

He shot her another sideways glance. Able to discern his face only by the lights from the glowing instrument panel, she couldn't read his expression.

But she recognized sarcasm when she heard it through her headset. ''You stalked me because I'm so charming?'' he asked.

''Not exactly.''

''You stalked me because I have an irresistible body?''

''Afraid not.''

''You stalked me because I'm into incredibly hot, kinky sex?''

She chuckled. ''Now you've got it.''

It took him several moments to catch on that she wasn't kidding, that she'd meant every impossible word.

His lower jaw dropped, before he appeared to collect himself and closed his mouth. ''We're about to land. Why don't you wait until we're on the ground to explain?''

''Okay.''

''I have a feeling I'm going to need all my concentration on you.''

''That's what you promised,'' she replied.

ZANE LANDED THE CHOPPER on the landing pad, shut down the engines, then removed his headset. Before he'd even opened the door, Jon Blanche, the caretaker, strode out of the darkness. ''You have a good flight, sir?''

''Just fine. Jon, this is Toni. Toni, Jon.''

Jon held a cell phone toward him. ''I know you don't

like to be disturbed while you're on the island, but they said it's an emergency.'' Jon headed toward metal rings in the concrete with straps that lined up with the chopper's landing gear. ''Don't worry about the tie-downs, I'll take care of that as well as the suitcases. My Melly has fortified the kitchen, and the horses are waiting. If you won't be needing anything else, I'll be going once I'm done.''

Zane paid no attention. He held the phone to his ear, almost hoping that reception had been lost. He didn't want interruptions. He wanted to focus on Toni and his plans. But he couldn't dismiss all of his brother's obligations without causing suspicion. ''Yes?''

''It's Stephen.'' His brother's right-hand man reported through the almost static-free connection. ''Someone hacked into the computer system and changed our headlines. Reprimand Of Judge Advised is now Spanking Of Judge Advised. Heat Between The Storms is now Heat Between The Sheets. Saints Favored To Win is now Saints Cheat To Win.''

''Production caught the errors before the main run?''

''Yes. The errors no longer concern me, it's the sabotage. What do you want me to do?''

''Call the police. Can you hold down the fort until I get back Monday?''

''Don't you think you should be here?''

''Stephen, I have every confidence that you can handle the situation.''

Zane's mind raced through possibilities. The computer system had firewalls to protect them from hackers, yet someone had gotten in. Maybe from inside?

He couldn't help recalling that Toni had had free access to his secretary's computer for the better part of an hour. While they had passwords to get into the computer, his secretary could never remember them and had them printed on a card that she kept under the blotter on the desk. A little snooping and Toni could have found the codes. She'd certainly had the opportunity to break into their network, and, once in, anyone with typing skills would have the means to change a few headlines. But what kind of motive would she have?

He recalled that before they'd landed how she'd been about to confess why she'd been stalking Grey. She'd more or less admitted that she wasn't creating a scandal to increase store profits. Was she on a mission to ruin Grey's reputation or bring down the paper? She didn't seem to have a conniving bone in her luscious body, but he knew better. She'd already admitted to stalking him at Club Carnal, and again at his dinner with the mayor.

"What's wrong?" she asked the moment he ended his phone conversation. "Why do you need the cops?"

Was she worried about him? Or herself, because she feared the police would catch her?

And why didn't his suspicions of her complicity make him want her less? What was it about her that made him need to believe she was innocent? Her wide eyes that seared him through the darkness? The genuine-sounding concern that touched him like a caress?

"We had another break-in at the newspaper." He kept his reply deliberately vague, hoping that if she knew more, she might slip up and reveal her part in the matter.

She found him in the darkness and eased her hands around his waist. "Was anyone hurt?"

He hadn't told her that the damage was done on the computer, but if she'd made the alterations through his secretary's system, she'd already know the answer to her question—which she could have designed to throw him off track. He made a mental note to ask Stephen to try and trace the history on the secretary's computer.

He realized the evidence against Toni was all circumstantial. She might be exactly what she seemed, a desirable woman who cared about him. As much as he wanted to believe her concern was genuine, Zane's experiences with women led him to believe otherwise. His regular jet-set crowd might not be into sabotage, but the women he knew had grown up mostly spoiled by their rich daddies and mommies. Wealthy and busy people who threw money at their children instead of love often failed to teach their offspring ethics and morality. So the women Zane knew usually saw no harm in lying to achieve their goals.

From the first, Toni had seemed different, but he was going more on instinct than experience. And with the newspaper at stake, no way could he trust her, not even enough to reveal his real first name, his true identity. For now, he'd continue to be Grey and keep his suspicions to himself. No point in confronting her openly, because if she was guilty, she'd only deny her treachery and be more careful.

"No one was hurt. And I don't want to think about business." He held her close, and she responded by leaning into him, as if sensing his intentions, arching her neck, so that when he dipped his head, their lips met. She didn't hesitate or hold back this time, parting her lips, her arms winding around his back, holding him tight.

At the sudden heat flash, he groaned. One kiss and his thoughts spun. That he wanted her while he suspected her of treachery didn't bother him. She could do little harm to the business on the island and he might learn a good deal if she slipped up. More accustomed to going with the flow than analyzing his own actions, he didn't alter his plans. However, his plans didn't include ravaging her right here on the chopper's landing pad, no matter how much she tempted him. He intended to ease her into lovemaking slowly because when they finally came together, he wanted her mindless with need.

He found the strength to break their kiss and step back. In the moonlight, he couldn't see her, but he heard her hitched breath which matched his own. Forcing himself to ignore his arousal, he drew oxygen deep into his lungs.

''Come.'' He took her hand. ''I have a surprise for you.'' He led her from the helicopter pad down several steps toward the stable, eventually regaining control of his anatomy. ''How do you feel about a midnight ride?''

''That's why I came,'' she told him, and he realized she'd misinterpreted his words. And after that sizzling kiss, he couldn't blame her, but thought he'd have a little fun before setting her straight.

''I was talking about riding Samson,'' he replied, using his amusement to cool the heat she'd kindled.

''Samson?'' She chuckled, obviously mistaking his reference to his horse for part of his anatomy. ''You don't think you might be exaggerating?''

''Samson's a stallion.''

''I'm sure he is.'' She giggled. ''And when do I get to meet Samson?''

''Right now.'' He flicked on the light. ''He likes to eat carrots.''

''Carrots?'' She looked around the immaculate stable, her gaze settling on his black horse with astonishment. ''Samson is a horse? You were talking about riding a horse?'' She broke into a delighted chuckle. ''I thought—''

''I know what you thought,'' he teased.

Jon had left several carrots by the feed bag, and Zane picked one up and placed it in her fingers. ''Hold your palm open, and he'll eat right out of your hand.''

Seemingly without the least bit of trepidation, she offered the carrot. ''That tickles.'' Toni patted the horse's neck and scratched him behind the ear. ''I've never ridden a horse before.''

''He has a smooth gait and adores swimming, although we'll save that for another time.'' Zane fed the animal the last two carrots, then slipped a bit into the horse's mouth and the halter over his ears before handing Toni the reins. ''This is going to be a ride we'll never forget.''

He placed a saddle pad with stirrups over Samson's back, then tightened the girth. Next, he placed a clean linen sheet on top of the saddle pad, wondering how long it would take for her to think about—

''I can't ride in a dress.'' Disappointment filled her tone. ''I don't suppose you thought to—''

He flicked off the lights and took the reins from her hand. ''I thought you could ride without the dress.''

''You want me to ride naked—like Lady Godiva?'' Her tone reflected more astonishment than outrage.

''We have the island to ourselves.'' He led Samson out of the stable. Obediently, Samson followed, his tail swishing. ''And it's dark.''

''What about Jon and his wife?''

''They have their own cottage and won't be up until morning.'' Zane held his breath. He had a backup plan.

In case she said no, there were all sorts of clean riding clothes in a locker back in the stable.

She didn't take long to make up her mind. "Fine. I'll agree on one condition—wait, two."

"And what would they be?"

"First, I get to keep my scarf." Zane eyed the strip of silk edged with glassy beads. His mind reeled with devilish possibilities. "Absolutely. Next?"

"I get to take off *your* clothes," she demanded.

"Agreed." Pleasure at her willingness to be daring filled him. "Now, turn around and let me unzip you."

For a moment, she appeared to have second thoughts. "I've never been outside without any clothes."

"It's scandalous," he encouraged her. "Not to mention invigorating. The breeze on bare skin is sheer freedom."

She kicked off her shoes, then gave him her back and held up her hair. Slowly, he tugged down the zipper, giving her every chance to change her mind. She didn't.

In the moonlight, the fabric slowly parted to reveal her pale skin, the graceful curve of her back and a slender waist. He sucked in his breath in appreciation. Bathed in moonlight, she reminded him of a wood sprite or nymph out of a fairy tale—but there was nothing childlike about her demeanor. Mysterious shadows and lush curves, she was all woman, enticing and compelling.

Her dress fell past her hips to reveal nicely rounded feminine buttocks. And when she wriggled her hips to step out of the dress, then strolled to the fence post to hang it up, his mouth went dry. Then she boldly strode back to him, clad only in moonbeams, the scarf dangling from her fingertips, her hips and pert breasts swaying with feminine allure.

When she reached for his shirt, he stepped back out of her reach. "Let me look at you."

She grinned at him, her teeth white in the moonlight. She wrapped the scarf around her neck, allowing the long edges to fall across her breasts, not so much hiding them but providing a delicious contrast of dark silk over pale skin. "What do you see?"

"Secret shadows. Enticing curves. Legs long enough to wrap around my waist."

"Now that's an image to stick in my mind." She reached for him, again. "Now, it's my turn to undress you." She stepped close enough for him to get a whiff of the clean scent of her hair.

"Not yet," he insisted.

"What do you mean, not yet?"

"I said you could undress me. I didn't say when."

She gasped, then for a long, tense moment, she remained completely silent. "You want me to ride naked while you remain clothed?" She tilted her head. "Why?"

At least she hadn't just blurted no. She had enough control to ask for his reasons, and he admired that she could keep so much dignity when she stood there so vulnerably naked on his island.

In return, he was honest. "I don't want to forget myself, and take you too soon," he admitted.

She shook her head. "No dice, cowboy. I won't do naked alone."

She wouldn't give him any slack. So they would be riding skin to skin. At the thought, his forehead beaded with perspiration.

She didn't wait for him to agree. She simply reached

up and unbuttoned his shirt. Slowly. She made a big deal of fingering each button, of easing back the material, of skimming her fingers over his bared chest.

And all the heat from their kiss flooded back until he wondered if he was going to be able to mount the horse without doing permanent damage. She reached for his slacks, unbuttoned and unzipped. ''And now I learn whether you prefer boxers or briefs or... Nice assets.'' She grinned. ''Nothing at all, huh?''

Before she could touch him and make mounting the horse even more difficult, he stepped away.

''Now, who's in a hurry?'' she teased, eyeing him with appreciation that made him glad he'd gone to the trouble of bringing her here. On the island, he could more easily be himself and give up the pretense of being Grey. The island might belong to his brother, but lately Zane had visited more often, making this his retreat from loud parties and mindless chatter.

Samson bobbed his head up and down and pawed the ground. Zane scratched him behind the ear to calm him.

Zane loved this island. Here, he would feel free to express himself with actions and show her how good the sex could be. She'd stirred his blood to a fever pitch by merely taking off her dress. But it wasn't just her body that had him eager and ready to show her a good time. He appreciated her attitude. She didn't play shy or coy games and made no bones about finding him attractive. He liked her spirit. Especially when she glanced from Samson to him, cocked her hip and teased, ''I suppose Samson is impatient?''

''He hasn't been ridden in a while,'' he agreed, wondering if he should take her into his arms and forget the romantic moonlight ride. But he'd promised her a scandal....

And the thought of riding with her spurred him on. He placed his foot into the stirrup and swung onto the saddle pad, then carefully eased himself into a sitting position.

He held out a hand to her. "Ready?"

7

TONI HAD NEVER BEEN LESS ready in her life. Nevertheless, after Grey freed his foot from the stirrup, she put hers there. They joined hands and his strong boost propelled her upward, and then she placed her leg over the saddle pad in front of him, careful not to kick him or the horse.

He'd previously adjusted the stirrups to fit his long legs, and after she settled between his hard thighs, her bare feet dangled free. She'd never felt so bold and reckless and vulnerable at the same time. His hard thighs around hers gave her a heady feeling and his jutting sex nestled in the curve of her bottom reminded her that she was probably in for the ride of her life. He placed one hand around her exposed waist to steady her, and she suddenly realized how completely he had access to her. All of her. Even while wearing the scarf, Grey could play with her breasts. Without any other clothing, with her thighs straddling the horse's back, Grey could touch her most intimate places.

Which was what she wanted.

So naturally, he paid no attention to her state of undress. Damn him.

He simply nudged Samson into a walk, finding a path through the pine trees. Without a bra, her breasts swayed deliciously free. Her scarf fluttered, tickling and teasing her skin. His powerful arm against her tummy seemed so close to going where she wanted him to go and yet so far.

Toni squirmed her bottom against his hardness, trying to turn him on so much he'd stop teasing her. But Grey had remarkable self-control.

The silver sheen of moonlight glinted out of the night sky, casting a spectrum of gray and black shadows and lending the seaside wildness a delicate air of limbo. They rode the path between scattered willows and live oak that grew horizontally. Beyond the numerous trees were cattails waving in the gentle breeze.

Since landing on the island, Toni had yet to spy the Gulf of Mexico, but she breathed in the salty tang from the sea breeze along with the smell of horse and the faint masculine aroma that Grey alone possessed. Her body tingled every time his bare chest rocked against her back, reminding her that she wore only skin and her filmy scarf.

A snowy egret soared overhead. When she tilted her head to watch the bird's magnificent flight, Grey leaned forward and nipped her earlobe, his earthy breath fanning across her neck. She shivered with delicious anticipation.

"Cold?"

She shook her head. "I feel scandalous."

"Scandalous good? Or scandalous bad?"

"That depends."

"Depends on what?"

"On what happens next."

"Have I let you down yet?"

"You haven't done *anything* yet," she reminded him, not bothering to hide her complaint, nudging her bottom against his erection.

"Oh, I wouldn't say that. I've got you on my private

island, captured between my thighs, wearing no more than a scarf. Any regrets, so far?"

Rubbing against him hadn't aroused him enough to stop teasing her. Perhaps her words might. "You haven't touched me yet—not intimately."

The erotic motion of the horse combined with his chest rubbing against her back made it almost impossible for her to think of anything besides making love. She recalled how hot he'd made her in the restaurant and how he'd pulled back. And now, if possible, she was even more eager for him. Despite her new and unusual surroundings, she couldn't stop thinking about when he was going to touch her, where he was going to touch her, and how he was going to touch her.

"I regret that, too. But I'm taking my time."

His soft words made her mouth go dry. He sounded so cocksure, so controlled, that a tremor of jittery expectation and apprehension flowed through her.

"So, we're going to enjoy the ride, see where we end up?" She drew in air and let it out slowly to calm her skittish nerves. "How long before Samson gets tired?"

Grey chuckled. "He'll outlast both of us."

He spoke with the certainty of experience. She supposed it would be unreasonable to assume that he'd never brought a woman here and ridden double on Samson. She turned and glanced up at his face. In the moonlight, he looked taller, his shoulders broader, his face harsher. Just a tad unsure of herself, but determined to follow through with her line of thought, she observed him closely to see if he'd try to evade her next question. "You've done this before?"

"Not with you."

His direct response without the slightest bit of hesitation heartened her and shot a shiver of anticipation straight to her core. That she wanted to make love to this man, she could not deny. She'd made that decision long before she'd agreed to fly to the island with him, before she'd taken off her clothes, before she'd agreed to follow his lead. Any man who could arouse her to this level of excitement wouldn't disappoint her. She'd been ready to make changes in her life, to allow more time for passion. And now that her goal was so close to being reached, she would never forgive herself if she didn't go for it.

As he skimmed his fingers from her tummy along her rib cage and under her breasts, her thoughts centered on the moment. She was riding a horse with her lover in the moonlight, without clothing, with his hard thighs wrapped intimately around her. The setting couldn't have been more perfect. He couldn't have been more perfect.

Her breasts responded immediately to his touch, aching, surging, her nipples hardening. She found herself holding her breath and had to remember to breathe. His fingers applied no more pressure than a feather, dusting lightly and leisurely and causing tiny goose bumps to break out on her skin.

"Actually, I haven't been out here in years." Casually, he tweaked a nipple. She gasped with pleasure and allowed her hands to drift to his thighs to steady herself. He chuckled and gifted her other nipple with the same treatment. "I'm glad you're having a good time."

She dug her fingers into strong thighs corded with muscles and swirled with fine soft hair and wished she could reach more of him. "I feel decadent."

"What else?"

''Wanted.''

He cupped both breasts and continued to tease her nipples. ''Oh, I'm wanting you all right.''

Samson kept walking, apparently not needing much guidance from his rider to follow the well-worn trail. And she found her hips rocking with the horse's pace, creating a tightening deep in her belly, and she hoped her rhythmic movements would cause him to lose some of his delicious control.

He pinched her nipple just slightly harder, rolling the tip between thumb and forefinger. ''Toni, to me, this is pure heaven.''

She let out a soft moan. ''You can't keep doing that to me.''

''Why not?''

''Because...'' She squirmed.

He placed the reins on his thigh. Samson stuck to the trail so Grey had free use of both hands, and he held on to her by her nipples, plucking and tugging even harder. ''Because why?''

All of the sensation in her body seemed to have centered in her aching breasts and between her legs. Her squirming against him had only served to increase the heat. And he seemed in no more of a rush than he had before.

''It's hard to describe.''

''Try.'' He massaged her nipples with his palms, coaxing her, teasing her.

''My stomach is fluttering. Every muscle is tight. Tense. Sensitive. Ready to explode with just the slightest encouragement. Only...''

''Only what?''

''You aren't going to make me come, are you?''

She already knew that he could keep up his arousing

caresses for far longer than she could stand to wait. And yet, she had to admit, while he took his time exploring, she was having a very good time, enjoying his soft taunting challenge and noting that each sensation was almost like a direct dare to grab the pleasure that was within her reach.

She tipped back her head and turned. When he bent close, she nipped his neck, then whispered into his ear. "Take me now, Grey."

"You're going to explode," he promised, his voice as smooth as satin. "Just not yet."

He removed his hands from her, and she took the moment to recover. However, her nipples remained hard and more sensitive than she'd known was possible.

Without warning, he snatched her scarf, then rearranged the material so that the glass beads along the edge dangled directly over her nipples. The crystals, heavy and shaped like diamonds, slapped, pinched and teased.

The jewelry was cold and hard, yet exhilarating, as if dozens of tiny fingertips toyed with her sensitive skin.

"What a perfect accessory. Now your breasts won't feel neglected when my hands move on to explore the rest of you." He chuckled.

Already tight, and oh-so-responsive, her nipples were so erect that she hadn't thought they could jut out any farther. But thanks to Grey's rearrangement, the beads had her taut and swollen, stirring a deep ache for more of his touch.

"I don't know if I can stand—"

"You in any pain?"

"Of course not. But—"

"Then you can stand it," he said so simply that she would have gotten angry—except what he had done to her felt so damn good.

And he *had* promised to use his hands on the rest of her. Never had she needed a man to touch her damp folds like she did right now. Never had she wanted so much to urge a man to hurry. But the horse's rocking movement combined with the night air on her bare skin and the dangling scarf and beads had drawn her into one edgy ball of need. She was wet, slick between her thighs, open and ready for him.

He was nibbling her neck, his tongue caressing the delicate shell of her ear. Maybe if she knew how long she would have to hold out, the waiting would be easier.

"Grey?"

"Hmm."

"How long is this going to take?"

"As long as it takes."

She groaned at his non-answer and bit her lower lip to keep from whining. After all, she had absolutely no right to complain. She had stalked him from the start, and he'd explained his intentions up-front, then given her every opportunity to change her mind. She would attempt to hold back her impatience. She just hadn't foreseen how exceedingly difficult slowing the pace would be.

He'd picked up the reins and steered Samson toward the left fork in the path, past reeds and tall grasses. Then they suddenly broke out of the trees onto a silver ribbon of beach. Waves gently lapped the shoreline and the moonlight glinted on the rippling sea.

He dropped one hand and teased his fingers up the

inside of her thigh. "Did you know some theories about bird migrations go back thousands of years?"

"Really?" The only migration she was currently interested in was the migration she hoped his hand would make to the place that strained for his touch.

"Primitive peoples believed birds flew to the moon for the off-season."

"Uh-huh." He'd settled the reins on his thigh, allowing Samson to make his own path down the shoreline. And while Grey repeatedly caressed her sensitive inner thighs, she tried to hold back a demand for him to hurry, but the exquisite sensations of his hands and the tantalizing massage of her breasts from the dangling beads made sitting still almost impossible.

"Aristotle believed that one kind of bird transmuted into another."

"Too bad Samson here can't transmute himself into a bed," she muttered.

He ignored her, but dipped his long fingers into her curls, sifting and combing, exploring every single centimeter of sensitive flesh. "And the most popular ancient theory held that birds, like bears, hibernated for the winter."

"Please, no more about birds...unless you want to talk about the birds and the bees."

He chuckled. "Distracted?"

"Impatient."

"For what?"

"Chocolate," she replied with sarcasm to prevent herself from begging.

He traced the very tip of her outer lip with his index finger, opening her sex, his caress so soft and subtle that she felt tense and jumpy...and cherished.

"If you're thinking about sweets, then I'm not doing

my job properly. Perhaps we should start over.'' He withdrew his hands.

''What?''

He traced the line of her shoulder with his jaw. ''I could take it from the top and work my way down again.''

He couldn't. He wouldn't. But he had already withdrawn his hands. And he was snacking on her shoulder as if he was a tiger lapping up a treat of sweetened milk. Damn him, he was beginning his seduction all over.

Damn. Damn. Damn. She wouldn't be this impatient if she didn't want him so much. She was already so sensitive. So ready. And if he wasn't going to pleasure her, she saw no reason not to please herself. She released her grip on his thigh, fully tending to ease her own need.

''Don't.'' As if anticipating her move, he nipped her shoulder, not painfully hard but certainly enough to gain her full attention.

For the moment, she moved her hand back to his thigh. ''Why not?''

''Because.''

''That's not good enough.''

''Because I want to give you that pleasure.''

''Well, then, by all means, don't let me deny you. Go ahead.''

''I plan to.''

Just not yet. The slightest stroke, just the tiniest pressure on her clit would be enough to send her over the edge. She knew it. Apparently, so did he.

''I really wasn't thinking about food, you know,'' she backtracked.

"Uh-huh." He nuzzled her neck, and her breasts ached, her entire body thrummed with need.

"I just didn't want—"

He played with the tips of her nipples and she wondered if she might come from those exquisite sensations.

"Didn't want what?" he prodded.

"—to admit how much I need your touch. Can't you go back to what you were doing?"

"You mean kissing your neck?" he teased.

"Damn you."

"I thought you understood that—"

"I didn't know waiting could be this hard. Don't you want to make love?" She leaned back and felt his erection press against her bottom. When she'd removed his pants, she'd gotten an impression of massive size, a hearty width and an enticingly musky scent. Now, from the feel of him nudging her, he seemed even larger. Apparently his toying with her had left him stoked… and yet he held back.

"We're going to make love," he promised.

Just not yet, he would tell her again if she tried to rush him. She gritted her teeth as his hands once again cupped her breasts, leisurely, lightly, lovingly.

"I'm doing you a favor," he told her, quite certain of himself.

"And I'm going to reciprocate this favor," she promised, her words ending on a gasp as he nudged Samson into a trot. A pace so different from the easy walk that it took several moments to adjust to the bouncing. While the horse trotted on, seemingly uncaring of the antics of his riders, Grey reached between her open thighs and cupped her with one hand, delving his fingers inside and around her lips, sliding into her wet heat with every bounce Samson took.

The friction between her thighs drove her to distraction. And all the while the beads teased her breasts, arrowing heat strikes straight into her heart. Her bottom pumped and repeatedly brushed against his cock and she did nothing to prevent the contact. She hoped the friction drove him wild enough to lose some of that control he seemed so determined to hang on to.

"Don't come," he pleaded in her ear, his fingers frantic as they kindled a blaze so hot, that she yearned for fierce release with every atom of her being. "Not yet."

Wind whipped her hair and her eyes teared. She'd never experienced anything quite so breathtaking and elemental. With the horse under her, Grey's fingers buried inside her and his breath fanning her neck, she almost screamed out in frenzied pleasure.

But then he slowed Samson back to a walk, moved his hands from between her parted thighs to her waist and lifted her above the saddle pad. Dangling in the air above the horse, she immediately missed Grey's warmth, the contact of his flesh heating her.

His voice—harsh from either the strain of holding her, or from excitement—rasped in her ear. "Put me inside you."

She didn't need any coercion, simply wondered if making love on a horse was possible. She'd never thought about such a stunt, but with Grey, the extraordinary seemed not only possible, but all-too-probable.

She reached down to him between her parted legs and, to her surprise, found he'd already encased his sex in a condom. Slick, hard and as ready for her as she was for him, he lowered her slowly onto him. Damn, he felt good, stretching her, filling her. But she hadn't quite figured out the logistics of making love on a horse. A living, breathing, moving horse.

"Place your thighs over mine, your feet on top of mine," he directed.

And, suddenly, all the parts fit perfectly. She could ride him while they both rode the horse. With her feet resting on his, she now had leverage to raise and lower her hips with ultimate freedom and abandon.

Moving experimentally, hands resting loosely on her thighs, she tested her position and drew a husky moan from Grey's throat before he choked out, "You okay?"

"Never better." She pumped her hips slowly, enjoying the feel of every terrific inch of him, timing her moves with the horse's natural rhythm.

"Why don't we see who can hold out longer?"

What? How could she think with myriad sensations bombarding her? He had filled her to her limit, his hardness stroking her softness and creating wondrous excitement. She couldn't wrap her mind around his suggestion and make sense of it. "What are you saying?"

"I'm...saying...that I can wait longer than you to come."

"You sure about that?"

Wicked and wild to prove him wrong, she tightened muscles that clamped around his sex. When he let out a gasp of delight, she repeated the movement, enjoying the feel of him, enjoying his enjoyment, too.

"With you," he bit out in a low rasping growl, "I'm not sure about anything." She would have grinned at his declaration, but she was desperately trying to hold back, trying not to let her senses overload as she listened to the challenge in his voice. "Why don't we make this more interesting?'' he dared her, one hand caressing her breast, the other reaching for her clit, finding her and teasing her mercilessly.

More interesting? Oh, sure. She was going to explode any second, and he wanted to make this more interesting?

Her ears pounded, the blood rushing to her head in time to Samson's pace. All her muscles tingled, tight with need. Her breath drew in short gasps of air that didn't seem to have enough oxygen, while her stomach fluttered madly and her breasts throbbed. Yet, somehow, she dug deep inside and found the strength to hold on to her scrambled wits.

''What do you have in mind?'' she asked, sounding boldly feminine to her own ears.

''A wager.''

With his sex dipping into her, then teasingly withdrawing, with his fingers beating their own tattoo between her legs and her throat so tight she almost screamed, she knew better than to make any damn bet. Especially when Grey truly seemed to have the stamina of a Samson.

Biting her bottom lip to keep from crying out as he slowed Samson to a very slow walk, she fought for control. She wanted the horse to let loose and gallop. She wanted to race toward the explosion so close, yet so far, from reach. No doubt Grey wanted to go slowly to draw out the pleasure but the delay was pure torment. She had a suspicion that Grey knew exactly how far he could push her, that he knew exactly how close she was to falling off the edge—indeed, that he could cause her to lose their bet anytime he chose. And the thought that he could play her like a finely tuned instrument, heating her up, only to cool her down, so he could cause her to blaze even hotter, only served to make her wonder how the hell she had gotten herself here.

She wanted to say, *I'm not a betting kind of girl,* but instead she heard other brash words come from her lips. "I'll accept your bet."

He chuckled warmly in her ear.

"Now we need to define the stakes." Wanting to prove to herself she was up for his challenge, she wriggled and reached between her legs to cup his large, tight balls.

"I like a woman who plays dirty." His tone was harsh, elusive.

"I play to win." She rolled his soft skin against her palm, testing the weight of him, searching and finding the tender spots which made him drag in a sharp breath and tenderly bite her earlobe.

"We'll wager one night of pleasure," he told her in a voice that was more demand than question.

"Huh?" She didn't understand, but now that she caressed his balls, she found herself more settled and enjoying her own boldness much more than she'd expected. Exerting her feminine power and skill shot reckless thrills through her.

Waves lapped against the beach and occasionally she could hear a fish jumping out of the water. The horse strode along the shoreline, the Gulf waters up to his ankles. A plopping and sucking sound that was almost sexual accompanied his every step. Water splashed his hooves as he carried his riders down the wide moonlit beach, a shoreline too primitive for a fancy resort brochure but one which suited her high-strung mood.

Grey's lips brushed, taunted and teased her temple. As she pumped her hips, his sex thrust in and out of her, creating heat that his clever fingers kindled into a raging inferno.

His provocative baritone titillated. "The winner gets a night of pleasure."

With every nerve ending excited and ready to fire, she couldn't possibly be thinking clearly. Either that or he was making no sense. He'd said the winner would get a night of pleasure but that couldn't be right.

He urged the horse into a quicker pace. The beads dangling on her nipples beat faster, as did his fingers rubbing more urgently against her clit, and all the while his cock pumped in and out. She was going to explode any moment.

Still, she gasped. "Doesn't the loser get a night of pleasure, too?"

"Yes."

"But—"

As if sensing her hesitation, he pressed. "A sexual wager would certainly be scandalous."

A scandal. Yes, she'd intended to create a sexual scandal. Oh, Lord. She must have been out of her mind. She couldn't keep up with this man. She was so ready to come, and he sounded as if he could last for hours.

The horse had angled his way into deeper water, maybe up to his knees. She welcomed the occasional splash like a thirsty woman crossing a desert plain. A few water droplets sprayed her breasts and dribbled down her stomach. She lifted her chin and stared at the sky. Limitless space. Countless stars.

And then she understood the logic of Grey's circular wager. "The winner and loser get the same thing?"

"Almost."

She found the big dipper and sighed her frustration to the heavens. "And the difference would be?"

He tweaked her nipple, already so tight that lust zinged straight through her like that first swallow of brandy on a rainy winter night. ''The winner decides on the pleasure.''

She might not be a betting kind of girl, but she didn't see how anyone could lose this type of bet. Of course, he was assuming they'd make love again, but that was just fine with her. ''Okay, I accept the bet and the stakes.''

She pumped her hips, this time letting her bottom brush against his stomach. The angle caused him to drive deeper into her, stretching her to take his full length. Damn, he was one finely built man. And that he was so determined to outlast her made her just as determined not to give in to the storm he'd created inside her.

But could she resist him?

8

TONI'S SENSUOUS CHANGE from sweetly acquiescent to saucily feminine had stirred Zane into a hissing, seething cauldron of sexual arousal. From the first time he'd met her she'd seemed a combination of innocence and brazenness that both surprised and intrigued him. If his little stalker had any idea of her awesome impact on him, she could have asked for the moon and he'd have given it to her. If he had his way, she could stalk him anytime and twice every other Sunday.

Every other Sunday? What in hell was he thinking? Zane adored making love with women, but he didn't do long-term, his previous record with one lady might be a few months. And he'd been thinking about Toni in terms that didn't fit into his idea of perfect.

But then how could he help himself when she seemed both so innocent and so brazen? She appeared to want nothing from him except what he was willing to give—which made her a very dangerous woman who attracted the hell out of him, excited him and inspired him to push her to see how far they could journey together.

He could barely believe that she'd never ridden a horse before, and now here she was riding naked, perched in front of him, her delectable backside rising and falling and taunting him, her blond locks whipping him to wilder exploits as her hand cupped him, her fingers dancing in delicious places. And he dared not move, dared not breathe.

He wasn't sure when the moment had happened, but somehow she'd wrested control from him. Samson might be *his* horse, riding along the shore of *his* family's island, and making love might have been *his* idea, but somehow, she'd made the notion her own. She'd gone from vexing to vixen, and now she held him captured between her legs, her core hot, tight and slick. She regulated their pace, she decided how much pressure to apply and when, raising and lowering herself, surrounding him, inflaming him, dragging him tighter and deeper inside her until he thought he would burst.

As he fought to hold back, sweat popped out on his brow and his pulse galloped raggedly. Each raw breath he drew into his lungs both energized and ached. He'd sought to distract her with conversation. But when she'd reached down and squeezed his balls, he'd almost accidentally dug his heels into Samson's sides. Not a good move.

His horse might be accustomed to midnight rides, but not with two riders, not with one of them raising and lowering herself onto him, causing them both to squirm. When she tightened her inner muscles to clamp down on his cock, he'd almost shouted in joy as the pleasure surged through him, seared him, branded him.

With the stars overhead, the ocean beneath Samson's feet splashing up the occasional spout of water, and the breeze on his bare skin, the lovemaking took on an otherworldly experience. Being inside her was so much more than sex—but he hadn't a clue why. And didn't especially care. Why ruin a good thing with overanalysis?

Sex had never been this perfect. And as her fingers

grasped and tugged, as she rode him, he simply closed his eyes and let the sensations take him to a place he'd never been. He had never felt so sensitive that he ached to crawl out of his skin, never been so swollen he thought he might burst before he was ready, never had his head gone numb.

His blood sang, pleading to increase the beat. He'd held back and held back and held back. But he couldn't hold out against such erotic pressures indefinitely. He was a man, and she was unlike any woman he'd ever come up against.

On the outside, she was pure supple softness driven by an inner core of feminine power, and the combination excited him. She maintained a feminine strength and intuition he hadn't guessed she'd possessed until now. Seemingly out of the humid air, she'd pulled out the knowledge of how he liked to be touched and where. He was beginning to think of his stalker as pure sorceress.

How else would she know exactly when to tighten her muscles around his cock? How else could she know that pressure under the rim caused his muscles to tremble clear up to the pit of his stomach?

Only determination to outlast her stood between him and a massive climax. Through aching jaws, he gnashed his teeth, frustration and desperation shooting through him like the compression of star gases before a universal explosion. Tilting back his head, he repressed a primitive howl.

Wet up to his knees, then his waist, he savored the cool spray. But when water sloshed over his hands that fondled Toni, he forced his eyes open.

They were a hundred yards from shore. Damn. He'd

failed to steer his horse and the animal loved to swim. Samson had set a course out to sea.

Water up to his waist, Zane floundered for the reins. Too late. The deepening water made reaching them impossible as they floated at a right angle. "Samson is set on a swim."

Before she could answer, he and Toni floated off the horse into the warm late-summer waters of the Gulf of Mexico. As they floated, Toni's muscles clenched in orgasm and her spasms of pleasure shot him over the edge. He poured into her and held on tight. She gasped in delight and clung to his forearms. For several long moments, he remained inside her, glad that neither of them could have delayed even one more second. But the mind-blowing floating sensation was well worth waiting for.

Satisfied and lazy, he regained his footing on the sandy bottom and wrapped his arms around Toni, sorry when he could no longer remain inside her. "You were wonderful."

"You weren't so bad yourself." Toni's clear laughter echoed across the water. "Talk about coitus interruptus!"

"I'm so sorry," he muttered, turning to watch his horse swimming onward without a look back. "He's not going to stop until he reaches the stable."

"How far is it?" She didn't sound terribly concerned and he enjoyed her adaptability.

"No more than a quarter mile of sandy beach. Hope you don't mind the walk."

"Let's see. A walk on a moonlit beach at night. On a private island. With a very naked, handsome and charming Grey Masterson. I think I can handle it."

He reached to take her into his arms and do what

he'd ached to do all evening. Kiss her. Her mouth welcomed him with a fervent ardor that told him more than words how much she was enjoying their evening. She tasted of salt and lemon lip gloss, a tangy combination that once again reminded him there was nothing simple about this woman.

She ducked underwater and came up with her hair flung back, looking as spectacular as a mermaid. Her teeth glinting in the moonlight, she splashed him, then ducked under again, disappearing before he could strike back.

He turned slowly, watching for her to resurface, ready to retaliate. So her hand on his ankle took him completely by surprise and yanked him off balance. He toppled, barely getting a breath before the water closed over his head. He didn't try to regain his feet but remained perfectly still, listening hard.

From his right side, either he sensed her movement or heard bubbles escape. Sculling with his hands to turn his position, then using a powerful kick off the bottom, he half swam, half glided, his body knifing through the water. Hands outstretched, he caught her shoulders with his fingers, let his hands slip to her waist and they both came up for air, bursting through the gently rippling surface and facing one another.

''You steered Samson out into the deeper water on purpose.'' She giggled, taking the sting out of her accusation. ''Didn't you?''

''And just why would I have done that?''

''To win our bet,'' she replied blithely.

Perhaps his more competitive twin might have pulled such a tactic to win, but laid-back Zane didn't care about winning or losing that much. He preferred to simply enjoy whatever moment he found himself living. Like this one, with a delightful companion who kept surprising him. She was just so different from other women he'd known. Perhaps he'd been choosing the wrong kind of women, or perhaps she was unique because she had seemed to enjoy delaying their pleasure as much as he had, willingly following his lead and pushing their senses to the limits. The wait and anticipation had paid off at a much higher rate than he'd expected. She'd known all the right moves, but responded to him in a way unique to his reeling senses. She was a risk taker. A sensualist. Yet, she was a career woman who seemed to have other priorities than growing her business. She was an innovative lover, as giving as she was needy. But never, ever greedy. If she was the saboteur, he'd bet a month's interest from his trust fund that she wasn't motivated by money.

But she'd just accused him of cheating. "I didn't need to resort to—"

"Oh, really?" She placed her arms around his neck and snuggled close, pressing her lush breasts against his chest, reminding him how responsive those breasts could be. "You were about to lose, dude. Admit it."

"Seems to me we both lost it at about the same time. In my book, that's a tie."

He thought about taking her again right here in the water. Zane might have made love to many women, but never without a condom. And he wouldn't take a chance with Toni, whom he'd come to admire so much. Taking her hand, he led her toward shallow water and the beach. "Seems to me that we both won."

"True. And you *were* terrifically inventive."

He had to admit that keeping her under suspicion of sabotage seemed silly after what they'd shared, especially since during their time together he hadn't found even one reason why she'd want to sabotage the paper. But there were still too many coincidences for him to ignore completely the circumstantial evidence against her.

And keeping his identity from her had begun to bother him, not simply the dishonesty, but his inability to be himself, having to temper his words, thoughts and deeds in deference to what Grey might say, think and do.

When they reached the beach, he continued to lead her above the high-tide line. Then he dropped to his knees and scooped out about twelve inches of sand, tossed the condom in the hole and buried it. "We try not to interfere with nature when we can," he explained. "Too many birds die needlessly trying to swallow manmade objects."

She stared down the beach and he followed her gaze. Samson had finished his swim, waded to shore and started a brisk canter toward the stable.

She chuckled. "And here I was worrying about Samson finding his way back in the dark."

He stood, brushed the sand off his hands, then took one of hers. Together, naked, they walked down the beach, as comfortable with one another as an old married couple. "Samson can't get lost on this small island. No matter where he goes, he'll smell his breakfast waiting for him and return."

"Are you saying Jon is already awake?" It was the first time since entering the water that she'd seemed the least bit self-conscious about her nudity.

He shook his head, and he explained as they headed toward the house. "The horse feeder is on automatic timer. That way if a storm kicks up while Jon's on the mainland and he can't get back here, Samson won't go hungry."

"And if a hurricane comes this way?"

"We move Samson inland by barge. Thanks to modern satellite forecasting, we can keep ahead of the weather. Back in my grandfather's and great-grandfather's times, they weren't always so lucky."

"You're lucky the island didn't wash away."

"The island's highest point is only fifteen feet above sea level, but, heck, New Orleans is below sea level."

He kept walking at a steady pace, and the gentle breeze dried the water from their skin, leaving him refreshed, clean and not the least bit sleepy. Sure enough, as they took a shortcut across the point along a sandy path, he spied Samson cropping grass by the stable, pawing the ground and shaking his head, impatient for Zane to remove the wet saddle blanket from his back.

Samson neighed a greeting, walked over and nuzzled him. Zane stroked the horse's neck. "He looks so sweet."

She scratched behind his ear. "You think he deliberately dumped us?"

"He most certainly did." Zane unstrapped the girth, removed the wet saddle blanket and sheet, then laid it over the fence rail to dry out once the morning sun rose. He removed the halter and reins, carefully dried the tack with a soft chamois, then hung the hardware back where it belonged inside the stable.

He returned to Toni to find her holding her dress and shoes, seemingly reluctant to put them back on. He'd retrieved clean robes from the stable and handed her one before snatching his shirt, slacks and footwear. He led her down a path she'd never seen, wanting to show her the place from the best angle.

She shrugged into the robe. "This leads to the house?"

"Yes."

"Can we watch the sunrise from there?"

Toni wanted to watch the sunrise.

Her words sang to him, the sentiment matching his own so perfectly that for a moment he just stared at her in wonder. Most women would be asking about a shower, breakfast, the sleeping arrangements or contemplating if they were about to step on a sandspur or be attacked by mosquitoes.

Toni wanted to watch the sunrise.

His heart leaped and he dipped his head down to take a quick kiss, almost to reassure himself that she was real and not some flight of fancy that his imagination had conjured out of thin air.

The way she simply dropped her shoes and dress by her feet and threw her arms around his neck showed him that she wanted him as much as he wanted her. Although both of them had experienced release, he wanted her again and she seemed to feel the same way. They'd found an ease together that was rare around people who had known one another for so short a time. However, that comfortable familiarity didn't mean that the sparks had gone out. On the contrary, those sparks could be kindled into a blaze with just a moment's notice.

Toni wanted to watch the sunrise.

His desire for her surged back, as elemental and relentless as the incoming tide. His cock rose with renewed life and urgency, demanding not to be denied. Maybe he responded to her so easily because he adored the way she kissed, feverishly, ferociously, foolishly wearing every emotion. She used her entire body, leaning into him so he had to support her. Her robe parted and she snuggled her breasts against his chest, her hard nipples ripe for his tongue.

But her nipples would have to wait until after he finished devouring her delectable mouth. Her lips fused to his, her tongue danced, frolicked and dipped, leading, then following and shooting his pulse sky-high.

The night had passed like the blink of an eye. At the very first lightening of the eastern sky, he knew that if he wanted to share this sunrise with her from his favorite perch, then they had to get a move on.

With a ragged pant he drew back and lightly swatted her very firm butt. "If you want to catch the sunrise from my favorite vantage point, we need to—"

"Okay." She pulled back, then kissed him again. "Okay, but don't forget where we left off."

As if that was possible. She had no idea what it felt like to stroll down the sandy path with his balls tight and full, his erection straining for release. Wanting her this badly reminded him how long it had been since he'd been this eager for a second time so quickly. Not since he'd been a teen and a walking hormone.

Now that he was older and more experienced, he was enjoying the waiting, the anticipation. Making love with Toni had already been one of the best encounters he'd ever had. And he was looking forward to exciting her all over again from scratch, to investigating not just every inch of flesh, not just where she liked to be touched, but what made her tick.

Perhaps even learning whether of not she was hiding other kinds of secrets—like a motivation for sabotaging the newspaper.

THE SAND PATH OPENED into a wide grassy area that sloped to a rounded point and the Gulf. With the house constructed at the island's highest point, the land swept downward toward the sea.

A C-shaped three-story home, constructed of layers of glass and stone balconies, bracketed a vast crescent-shaped screened enclosure. The multilevels of patios included a pool with a waterfall and whirlpool and extensive gardens in bloom. A soft lapping of waves against a seawall and the view outward drew her attention. The waters of the Gulf rippled, the tangy breeze a heady inducement to romance.

Toni, hand in hand with Grey, padded barefoot beside him as they climbed a half staircase that led to a higher view. The soft tinkle of flowing water accompanied their footsteps through the stepped garden levels.

"The top floor is my favorite," he told her. "We can grab some blankets from the master bedroom, if you're cold."

"I'm fine. Actually, I'm surprised by the lack of bugs."

"Tonight the onshore breeze is keeping them away, but that's not always the case. The island is full of no-see-ums and mosquitoes. That's why we screened in so much of the backyard."

They climbed one full flight of steps to a captain's deck off the master bedroom. The layout was unlike any building she'd ever imagined, the bedroom extending toward the sea, completely open to the elements.

"What happens when it rains?" she asked.

Grey showed her doors which interlocked and closed off the carpeted and wallpapered part of the room. Now blissfully open, the bedrooms seemed part of the landscape. Huge skylights let in the gleaming stars and caught moonbeams that reflected off shimmering black wallpaper.

But again the sea called to her, and she turned to explore the captain's walk, a deck that totally surrounded the master bedroom, allowing a 360-degree view of the island. From here she could see the stable, tennis courts, helipad, golf carts, a putting green and a boathouse.

Noting the direction of her view, Grey commented, "Tomorrow—make that later today—we can take out the personal watercraft, sail a catamaran, go fishing, or windsail. There's scuba gear and—"

She gasped, stopping in her tracks, and pointed. "What's that?"

He grinned. "My favorite spot."

"Your favorite spot is a trampoline?"

The workout area came with all the trappings: free weights, treadmills, butterfly machines and leg machines which took care of both inner and outer thighs. Tucked into a corner was a steam bath, sauna and his-and-her whirlpools, even a Japanese soaking tub. He walked over to a fully equipped kitchen, and extracted a plate of fruit, cheese and a bottle of chilled wine he'd earlier requested the caretaker's wife supply.

With food and drink, they strode back toward the perimeter, then climbed onto the trampoline and arranged a few pillows to tuck under their heads. Then he took the tray from her and balanced it on his stomach.

"Hungry?"

"I'm starved, but I've never eaten on a trampoline."

"It's good for lots of things."

"Uh-huh."

"Like stargazing."

"Uh-huh."

"We used to have a hammock here, but this is much more comfy."

He patted a pillow beside him. "Try it."

Losing the robe, she rolled beside him and let out a contented sigh. The webbed matting had some elasticity to it and was more comfortable than she'd have thought. Their heads ended up next to each other on one of the pillows, and they stared at the sky.

Without lights from a large city or the island, the stars shined brightly, giving them their own private show. The water made a slightly harsher sound than on the beach, the waves ricocheting from the seawall and combining with the flowing tinkle from the patio fountains. Rugged and elegant, the building surprised her, as did Grey.

From the book she'd read about him, he was supposed to be the man who held the family business together, the workaholic, the conservative one, the Mr. Business, the man with the don't-bother-me-with-anything-but-work ethic. But he certainly hadn't had any trouble letting loose with her—then again, according to Lane's book, he hadn't had trouble relaxing with the movie star, either.

Clearly he didn't like to discuss his parents or his brother, which she found odd. Most people enjoyed talking about themselves, finding the subject matter utterly fascinating. Grey acted as though he'd rather think of anything but his regular life. She wondered about his reasons, but didn't know him well enough to judge. She couldn't help hoping, though, that if she opened up to him, he might just reciprocate a little.

With the intimacies they'd already shared, it was important to her that they felt free to discuss their feelings about their family, their businesses and their lives. While she felt perfectly comfortable opening her body to Grey, she wanted to open up to him on other levels. And number one was sharing her reason for stalking him—something she'd meant to do before they made love the first time.

Grey plucked a piece of fruit from the plate and held it to her lips, allowing sweet juice droplets to tease her bottom lip. "Do you like pineapple?"

She opened her mouth, and he ever so slowly placed the tidbit between her lips. The tangy treat reminded her that she could use a meal to keep up her strength. After having spied Grey discreetly retrieving a condom from a cabinet, she figured he intended to use the trampoline as a bed. She hoped, anyway.

But food first. Her confession would be second, before pleasure, she vowed.

He fed her bite-size pieces of lobster, cheese, more pineapple, and green grapes. And they sipped their wine through bent straws, the kind that children use. Silly, but fun.

And whenever her hand brushed his hip or his fingers touched her thigh, the accidental contact became a caress, a delicate stroking that induced their need for more.

With the food demolished, Grey left her side to remove the empty plates to a nearby table. When he returned to the trampoline's matted padding, her entire body bounced as if they shared a floating air mattress. But the trampoline was better and bigger than any air mattress. There was no chance of flipping off into the water. One drenching a day was enough, thank you very much.

As the sun rose, all pink streaks and purple slashes on a band of yellow-gold sky, she figured both her confession and their lovemaking could wait just a few more minutes. Reaching out, she took his hand, eager to drink in every precious second of the rapidly rising sun in the fiercely blue dawn sky.

The back of the house faced the mainland where she could just make out on the horizon. Although there was land to the north, east and west, their immediate view was mysterious sea and sultry sky, the mainland much too far away to mar the spectacular view.

She held her breath at the steady chirps of crickets and the song of deep-throated bullfrogs. A hawk launched himself from a willow tree and soared proud and high over the eaves. She watched until she could no longer see him, realizing that he'd probably landed on another low-lying island for a rest before continuing his journey.

She was going to feel as free as that soaring hawk, she vowed to herself, even if it was only for a few hours. But her need to explain her motives to Grey and share her reason for stalking him increased in proportion to how much time they were spending together. She hadn't felt guilty about misleading a stranger, not when he'd had so much to gain in return. Grey's reputation had been restored, just by the press noticing him with another woman. By bouncing back with a new woman, Grey would only become that much more attractive as an eligible bachelor.

But Grey was no longer a stranger, and she'd come to care for him in ways she hadn't expected. He'd been considerate to offer her a robe, thoughtful to feed her, romantic to offer her this magnificent view of the sunrise. Perhaps it was his gentlemanly conduct, mixed with his rakish confidence, but she wanted this man to know she was stalking him for a much more personal reason than money. And she was wise enough to realize she wanted to tell him because she wanted him to like and respect her back—not necessarily a requirement for good sex, but definitely a requirement for a good relationship. And that's where she thought she might like to go. To freely jump in, give him her best, take what she wanted and see what happened. Normally, she wasn't so carefree. But then again, normally, she didn't hook up with men she read about in *Southern Tycoon Magazine.*

She laced both hands through his and sat opposite him on the trampoline mat, cross-legged so both their knees were touching. "There's something I have to tell you. I tried back on the helicopter, but then we had to land and I lost the chance."

"You came here because you're really my father's illegitimate cousin on his mother's side and want a share of the island?" he teased.

"That must be it. After I let you freely sample all my delectable charms, you'll simply sign over the island to me," she teased him back, but realized that his words clearly revealed his memory of their conversation right before the helicopter had landed. He must have been curious, yet he'd asked no questions, allowing her to reveal her reasons in her own way. Was he so patient a man? Or was it that he just didn't care enough to ask?

"Sorry, you can't be an owner." He gazed at her nudity appreciatively, the heat from his gaze searing her, and almost, but not quite, distracting her from the conversation. "A female can inherit only after she marries and supplies an heir."

"A male heir?"

"Of course."

She chuckled that he could so ably insert a measure of silliness into serious conversation. Clearly, he intended to befuddle her, but she wasn't letting him get away with such lame tactics.

"Well, let's see," he deadpanned. "If you didn't come to stake a claim to a false inheritance, perhaps you came to kill me?"

She frowned at him. "What would be the fun in that?"

"Well, you certainly don't mind torturing me," he teased.

Like he should talk after what he'd been doing to her ever since they'd met. And he still hadn't satisfied her craving. She wanted more of him and this was one man who deserved a payback—in spades.

She allowed her frown to turn upward into a grin. "Riding you was rather interesting."

His eyes glimmered with renewed heat. "So then I might persuade you to try again?"

"You might."

9

TONI EYED ZANE WITH mischief and an odd combination of need and hesitancy. "First, we need to talk."

With another woman, Zane's first inclination would have been to delay serious talking until after making love again. But with Toni, having her again wouldn't satisfy him. He wanted to know what was bothering her. He wanted to know what made her tick. He wanted to know everything about her.

Zane had known many women and didn't claim to understand everything about them. Some women's faces and thoughts were as clear as a four-inch headline. Others hid their opinions in the fine print. With Toni, he was willing to read the entire paper, front to back, to find out more about her.

Yet, every male instinct told him that what she was about to say could make him stop wanting her. He felt as though he was balanced on the edge of a cliff, where one precarious move could shove him over. The playboy in him struggled to fight down his own automatic reactions.

She wanted to talk.

And as much as he wanted to listen, he also ached to take her into his arms.

She felt the need for words.

He felt the need to be inside her.

One look into her earnest face and serious eyes told

him that any move to make love to her would insult such determination. Especially once he picked up the mixture of sadness and worry on her face, as if she expected her revelation to lead to his disapproval and rejection.

So he did his best to ignore her tanned skin that called to him to bite and suckle. Uncharacteristically, he ignored the burning need surging through his system and tried to tune his senses to her mood. It wasn't so difficult—after all, he was curious.

In the same situation, Grey might have been better able to keep his priorities straight. Business first. Talk first. Normally Zane was more inclined to allow his desires to take control. Desires that promised to blossom into exquisite, mind-numbing orgasms. But, with Toni, he had a genuine need to hear what she had to say. Besides, they'd already taken the edge off the humming tension between them, satisfied themselves in a way that would draw them closer together and, he hoped, make them better able to overcome whatever she now felt so compelled to tell him.

"I'm listening," he offered, prepared to hear her out with a patience that surprised him.

"I'm not sure where to start," she began softly, her tone making him ache with growing confusion, although he wasn't quite sure why.

"What's the problem?" He scratched his head, appalled she was so obviously reluctant to share her thoughts. He didn't like the idea that she would share her body more easily than what was on his mind—which had to be a first for him. "I thought we were doing just fine. Fine enough for you to talk freely with me."

"Fine?" Her eyes flared with aggravation. "And you're basing this keen observation upon what?"

"I thought..." Hell, he stopped, realizing his thoughts had been atypical since she'd stalked him right from the beginning. And when he'd taken her up on her offer, she'd been as eager as he to have a good time. If she hadn't wanted to talk now, he would have seen no reason not to make love to her again. He considered their little ride on his horse to be an appetizer for the main course, which would involve sampling the delicious pout of her full mouth and feasting on her delicate skin. But she seemed a little peeved with him, even though he'd put his lust on hold and agreed to hear her out.

"What's fine?" she grilled him. "The sex? Okay, I'll admit it, the sex is fine. The sex is great. Is sex all you want from a woman?"

"Sometimes," he admitted, then winced at the sound of his own honesty. Suddenly, wanting just sex made him seem shallow. He'd always believed sex was a need, right up there with the need to eat and to sleep. And there was nothing wrong with choosing to have only sex in a relationship. But with Toni, he wished he could just crawl right inside her head, figure out what she wanted and give it to her. Words were too slow and clumsy, but he told himself to be patient, careful.

She threaded her fingers through her hair. "Well, to tell the truth, I was hoping sex with you would be enough for me, too, but it's not. I want to share more—but if you're not into that, then I guess we're done here."

She was making assumptions that he was just discovering weren't true. Earlier, he may have acted as though sex was more important than getting to know her better, but, actually, he found himself quite curious to hear what she wanted to say. Obviously, his actions indicated otherwise and he needed to correct her impression.

Her voice, not the least bit accusing or hurt, had sounded matter-of-fact, a little melancholy and wistful perhaps, but not at all needy. She could and would walk away from him, right now, with some regret, but confident in the belief that they were incompatible.

But he needed to make sure he understood. "Let me get this straight, I'm not right for you because—"

"Without sharing our thoughts and feelings, there is no *us*. There's simply you and me and sex."

"Our lack of communication last night on the horse was pretty damn good," he teased, knowing she would get to saying what she needed to say in her own way, in her own time, well aware he'd just delayed saying the words she needed to hear. Since he'd never before admitted having these kinds of feelings, he hadn't realized how difficult admitting them to her would be.

With his reminder of their lovemaking, her eyes softened. "You swept me into a fantasy."

"Is that a complaint?"

"Of course not."

Knowing she would refuse him, but enjoying watching her struggle, and all the while curious as hell about what she was having so much trouble telling him, he offered, "I could do it again."

"If I allowed you to." She licked her bottom lip as if nervous.

"But you won't?"

"No. I won't."

"Did it ever occur to you that I want to hear what you have to tell me?" he asked, surprising himself by finally making the admission that left him exposed. "That I want to hear what goes on in that head of yours?"

"Seems to me, you'd prefer we just close out the rest of the world with mind-blowing lust."

"I admit I find that notion rather appealing."

"Me, too."

His eyes narrowed as he turned the tables on her. "But I'm insulted that you think I'm just interested in you for sex."

"Really?" Her eyes searched his with a glimmer of hope. "For me, the sex has got to lead somewhere."

"Where?"

"To genuine caring, a progression from acquaintance to friendship to love. Otherwise, I might as well take my vibrator to bed."

"Now there's a flattering thought." He grimaced. "And here I thought I was giving you what you wanted."

"You did, and being with you was terrific."

Was? He didn't appreciate the way she'd so easily relegated their relationship into the past tense. As if they were over and done before they'd gotten started, as if he hadn't just admitted to her that he cared what she thought. "Being with me is so terrific you want to leave?"

"So terrific that I want *more* than sex. I don't want to live in a sexual fantasy all the time, and despite what you just told me, I think that you do. I want the real world. The moles and the warts, the wrinkles and the tummy aches."

"Exactly what must I say to convince you that I want more than we had together last night?"

She cocked her head sideways, deep in thought.

"Sex with you was wonderful. We are in lust. But to stay in the same emotional place isn't right for me. Either we move forward or I cut my losses."

"And we aren't moving forward because—?"

"Because you substitute sex for intimacy. You say you're willing to listen, but the offer is simply a prelude to more sex."

How could she read him so well? They hadn't known one another long enough for her to make such sharp observations, but her insight had him reeling. She'd certainly pegged him. His normal way of looking at relationships had served him well up until now. And, obviously, although he viewed Toni differently, he wasn't acting differently enough for her to tell how special he found her. For her, he was going to have to change his modus operandi to match his inner feelings. For a moment he wondered if she was worth the effort. But at the idea of losing her, his determination hardened.

Toni was different from any woman he'd met. Letting her bail wasn't an option. Not when every lush curve of her had him hard and aching for relief. Not when he actually cared about her in a way that thoroughly confused him.

Where was his normal take-'em-and-leave-'em attitude? Why didn't he believe this woman could be replaced by another willing female? And, damn it, he wasn't one of those men who ran from intimacy, was he? He just liked to keep his private thoughts private.

And she didn't know how adaptable he could be. If a conversation would make the difference between her staying or bailing on him, then he would listen. Eagerly—not just to get to the sex, but because he wanted to know more about her. And for the sake of the family business, he would get to the bottom of the sabotage. Normally, he would have been much more interested in Toni's bottom, those feminine curves that had his hands itching to explore and stroke. But he thrust away his impulse to touch her with an ease that spooked him. He was willing to alter his behavior for her, change for her, because he wanted to know her better. Now, all he had to do was convince her.

"I've wanted to learn more about you ever since we met. So, okay. Let's talk. Tell me why you stalked me."

She frowned at him, clearly wary of his motives. "You're still hoping that we'll make love, aren't you?"

"Yes." He gestured to their naked bodies lying on the trampoline in the gleaming sunlight and grinned. "We seem appropriately dressed for the occasion."

"And suppose I said no? Would you still want to talk to me about why I stalked you?"

"I want to get to know you, Toni. Is that so hard to believe?"

At his answer, her lips parted in surprise and challenged his sincerity. "But why would you care, if there was no payoff for you?"

There would be a payoff, no doubt about it. If she believed otherwise, she'd didn't know him well. "The more you tell me, the more insight I'll have into what makes you tick. Then I'll know even better how to please you, and I'll use that knowledge to make love to you for the rest of today."

"Now, you're contradicting yourself." She shook her head and a lock of blond hair tumbled across her eyes. She smoothed it away and looked him directly in the eyes. "You just said you cared about what I think."

"True."

"In order to get laid? Or because you care about what I think?"

Since such an admission would reveal his growing feelings, he shrugged. He'd just admitted to himself how much he liked Toni. He liked her a lot. He liked her inherent honesty. He liked her passion for life. But most of all, he liked her self-confidence. She knew what she wanted and pursued her goals with an attitude that would never entertain failure. But admitting his feelings to her would bring him to a whole new level—one he'd never before scaled.

Zane might not know how to define exactly what he felt for this woman, but he couldn't let her just walk away. "Believe it or not, I'll enjoy our conversations. I'm not about to allow you to write me off as a total loss. And if sharing is important to you, then it's important to me, babe. Besides, you've aroused my curiosity."

She glanced to his straining erection. "That's not all I've aroused."

"He has a mind of his own. Talk."

"As long as you're willing to hear me out, I'm willing to compromise." She let her fingers stray from his knee up his thigh. "I don't see why we can't both get what we want. I can talk and play at the same time."

He took her words as a personal challenge. It would be interesting to see exactly how long they could keep their minds on conversation. But as her hand caressed his thigh, he was the one who had trouble keeping his thoughts focused on sex. He really did want to have answers to his questions. "So just when and why did you decide to stalk me?"

"The last man I dated believes we're engaged."

Zane reached for her chin and tipped her head up, looking directly into her eyes for the truth. Was she telling him another story? He cupped her lower jaw in his palm and made tiny circling caresses on her cheek. "You're engaged? When is the wedding?" He glanced over his shoulder, pretending to look for an angry fiancé about to pounce, but, in truth, he needed time to recover from the significance of her confession. That she was already tied to another man bothered him more than he'd expected. Zane considered himself a good judge of character, but Toni had confused him completely. She didn't appear to be a woman who would fool around on her fiancé or use Zane for one last fling.

"There's not going to be a wedding," Toni told him, her expression fierce, her tone sharp. "There never was."

She leaned into the caress of his palm and continued to stroke his thigh, causing heat to surge between his legs. However enticing her caresses, he knew she wasn't making sense, but her words and actions filled him with hope that she wasn't in love with that other man.

He needed clarification. "You're engaged, but aren't going to marry?"

"I said my friend *believes* we're engaged."

"Now why would he think that?" With his fingers, he traced a path down her neck, over her fragile collarbone and around her breasts. Her nipples hardened, two enticing rosebuds perking up at his attention.

"I don't know why he thinks we're engaged."

Hell, she still wasn't making sense. He hadn't realized how difficult having a discussion with her would be while he played with her silky flesh. With other women, he could let them talk but he never cared much about their words. With Toni, he wanted to understand, yet her soft hollows and lush curves kept distracting him as much as the surprising admissions she was making. Surely, he must have missed something since he didn't have a clue where she was taking this conversation.

He had difficulty keeping the confusion from his tone. "You don't know why he thinks you're engaged?"

Toni's hand teased across his skin, her fingers splaying in his chest hair. "He's stubborn and fixated on me."

"He sounds dangerous."

She let her hand drift lower to his stomach where she paused to explore his navel with her fingertip. "I assure you that in every other respect the man is normal. In fact, he's popular and quite handsome. Other women flock to him."

"But?"

"But he did nothing for me. His kisses left me cold. Unfortunately, *he* feels differently. When it comes to me, he thinks..."

"He thinks what?" Zane prodded as he tried to ignore the fabulous sensation of her fingers dipping below his waist. At the same time he felt quite satisfied that, while she didn't want this other man, quite clearly she felt differently about him. To distract himself from his rioting pulse and his ragged breathing, in turn, he played with her breasts, enjoying the way she arched into his hands.

She sighed, either in delight at his ministrations or in annoyance over the other man. "He thinks that I'm the perfect woman for him."

She *was* perfect. From the top of her blond head, to

her flawless satiny skin, high breasts, nipped-in waist, down her long, lean legs to her straight little toes, she was delectable. But it wasn't simply her body that turned him on. He was falling for her beautiful brain. Zane wasn't surprised that another man had pursued her so avidly. He figured it was only a matter of time before some guy convinced her to get hitched.

Not him, of course. He never intended to marry.

He'd always figured he'd leave the traditional duty of marriage and kids to Grey, never intending to fetter himself with such responsibilities. He enjoyed the freedom of his lifestyle too much to consider tying himself to one place, one job, or one woman.

So, in a way, Toni had been right when she'd accused him of living for the fantasy. Sex with the same woman, night after night, year after year, didn't appeal to him. He'd get bored. Besides, Grey was the twin who took the traditional path. Grey would supply their parents with grandchildren while Zane went happily about his free lifestyle. No problems. No regrets. No hassles. Mottoes he lived by.

Still, he found Toni's predicament disturbing enough to delay the gratification of kissing her. "Why does your fiancé think you're perfect?"

"He's *not* my fiancé. He's settled on me for his bride-to-be because my family is respectable. Because he knows my father and is about to offer my dad the job of his dreams. Because he thinks that while he works, my career will keep me busy and satisfied."

What a dreadful fate to befall this beautiful, sexy woman. If she were his, he wouldn't depend upon a business to keep her satisfied—not when there were other, much more pleasant ways to spend their time together, such at talking to her between bouts of love-making.

She couldn't have any idea how much he wanted to dip his head and taste her lips. Yet, he wanted just as much to hear the rest of her story. So, he both concentrated on her words and focused on upping her pulse rate by tracing her aureole, lightly, enjoying how it puckered in response. Instead of licking the tip, he asked, "So why don't you just tell him no?"

"I did." She heaved a sigh that shot her breast fully into his hand.

He didn't see the problem. No meant no. What was there not to understand? As he frowned over her answer, he was unable to resist licking the tip of her nipple and took immense pleasure in watching her flesh harden even more. "And?"

She skimmed her fingers along his straining sex, her expression thoughtful. "He sent me an engagement ring. I sent it back."

"That should have been the end of any notion of marriage."

She shook her head. "He practices selective hearing when I tell him no. I have no doubt that he simply thought I didn't like his ring, not the potential groom."

"Sounds like he has his technique down pat, but surely he has to understand your wishes?"

"He doesn't. And I would tell him off if there weren't two little problems. First, I'm afraid of setting back my father's career. And second, well, there's Bobby."

"Your sister?"

"She won't admit it, but I think she's sweet on him." She sighed. "On top of that, he's done a couple of favors for Mickey and Jude that he could just as easily take away.''

His brain might be fuzzy from desire, muddled by her story, but he could still put the pieces together. ''So you decided to back off?''

''Only nothing reasonable worked. My sister Mickey thought it might be better if the man backed away from *me,* so my sisters and I concocted a plan.''

''To cause a sex scandal?'' he asked, understanding warming him as much as her fingers gently teasing his inner thighs.

He trailed his hand down to her flat belly, then lower into her curls. Her flesh quivered beneath his touch, and he slowly parted her lips, anticipating dipping into her core. She was moist, slick, ready. He stopped his caresses for a moment, eager to hear her explanation.

She spoke in a rush, as if as eager as he to get out the story. ''I figured you were perfect. Your name had already been on the news due to Lane Morrow's book. And you're prominent in the city, so your seeing another woman would be food for the paparazzi. It was a win-win situation for everyone. Your reputation would be flattered since you would be dating another woman and not appear to be brooding about the loss of your former lover. And my fiancé would back out with his ego intact.''

Her plan, albeit outlandish, had merit. He could only admire her audacity. Yet, it still didn't all quite make sense. However he had to allow for gaps in logic due to his rapid pulse and skipping heart. ''Didn't he read the first newspaper article about us?''

She grabbed the base of his erection and began to stroke him slowly, seriously, seductively. ''He called to tell me he understood how the papers could turn the most innocent meeting into appearing like something more.''

''He made excuses for you?'' Zane shook his head, baffled by the man's reaction.

''He was going to call and thank you for protecting me from the press.''

As she moved her hand over him and let her thumb trail around the sensitive rim of his cock, he struggled to concentrate on conversation. ''No one ever called.''

He sank one finger into her heat and her eyes darkened with passion. When he found her G-spot and focused his pressure there, he watched her struggle to maintain control. But the telltale bounce of the trampoline gave away her heightened state of arousal. Holding still was becoming more and more difficult for her. Good.

Still, she kept circling her fingertip, her palm stroking him to an even greater size. She seemed to know exactly what kind of effect she had on him, offering him a tight smile. ''When he actually put out a press release about our engagement, then sent that ring a week later, I was so horrified I had to take drastic measures. That's when I borrowed the gorilla suit and tried to gain your attention.''

So Toni wasn't guilty of sabotage at all. Her reasons for being with him were much more personal, much more to his liking. He shouldn't have doubted her.

And Zane liked her drastic measures; after all, they'd worked out to his benefit. ''So you were strictly pursuing me to cause another man to back out of your engagement?''

''That was my initial reasoning. Yes.'' In contrast to their nudity and their intimate stroking of one another's bodies, she spoke almost primly. ''But the more I got to know you, the more time I wanted to spend with you.''

''I'm glad.''

''I can see that.'' Her nails trailed deliciously along his length. ''I've been spending too much time on business and now I'm ready to devote more time to pleasure.''

He grinned and spoke teasingly, but he couldn't keep the husky need from his tone. ''A woman after my own heart.''

''Take warning, Grey Masterson, that's exactly what I'm after—your heart.''

Despite his eagerness to plunge into her, her words gave him a moment of anxiety. First, her calling him by his brother's name gave him pause. And, second, she'd stated her goal easily, casually, yet with a determination that warned him she would not be deterred. He supposed over the years other women had wanted him to fall in love with them, but he'd always escaped. And this time would be no different. He would take what she offered, give her pleasure in return and then send her on her way before he became any more attached to her.

He hadn't lied to himself or to her when he admitted that he cared about her. He did. But he needed to move on. She'd admitted to becoming serious about him. And he needed to break away soon to let her down easy. He didn't want to hurt her. But he didn't do serious relationships.

And since he no longer believed she was guilty of sabotage, he was free to return to his own life and his old ways. She was not the saboteur. It had been a coincidence that the oil had ruined the ink while she'd distracted Grey in her gorilla suit. And probably just bad luck that the sand had been placed in the oil tanks while they'd been at Club Carnal. Anyone could have found the codes in his secretary's desk and gotten into the computers to alter the headlines. She'd simply been a stranger who'd come into his life during a crisis. He didn't have one shred of hard evidence to link her with the sabotage and he wasn't about to blame her on circumstantial evidence. Her story was too crazy to have been concocted just as a cover. She had to be innocent.

Now that he realized that she probably had nothing to do with the sabotage at the paper, there was no reason to spend more time with her. He would allow himself the distraction of her wonderful company for the afternoon, but tomorrow he would end their time together. The thought saddened him. Her loss would leave a void, one he would deal with tomorrow—and one which he needn't think about while he could feel her slick heat trapping his finger, her muscles clenching him, spasming ever so slightly while her eyes glazed with desire.

He had no intention of allowing her to slip over the edge. Not yet. Not when he could ease her down and then start all over again. He stopped his fingers from moving, drawing her attention from wherever she'd been. She blinked, taking in the view of the ocean, the gulls soaring and cawing, finally centered on him.

"You felt so good. Why did you stop?" Her tone, sexy and low, scraped over his raw nerves.

Sensing how good the sex between them could be, he wanted to prolong her heightened state of arousal as long as he could hold out. Sweat beaded on his brow but he answered her in a measured tone. "There's no rush."

She licked her bottom lip then glanced from his erection to his face. ''There's no reason to wait.''

Slowly he wriggled his index finger against her, but this time he slid his thumb up to find her clit. As he slowly caressed her most sensitive spot, her eyes widened and her pupils dilated. ''Waiting, watching you, makes me a happy man.''

''I could make you happier,'' she offered, reaching for the condom he'd set out earlier.

He caressed her, using tiny circling strokes of the pad of his thumb. Her breathing grew irregular and she fumbled with the foil packet.

''I need to…need to open…''

The packet slipped from her fingers and floated through the trampoline's webbing to the decking beneath. Although he had several more condoms, he withdrew his hand from her once again and frowned at the packet, glinting on the deck beneath them.

A lock of hair fell across his forehead and into his eyes. Hoping she wouldn't guess his intentions, he muttered, ''If you turn over, you can probably scoop it back up.''

Without hesitation she scooted to the edge of the pillows and leaned over the edge at her waist. She couldn't reach the condom, of course, but now he had her trapped. It took only a moment to move between her thighs and effectively pin her.

''I can't reach,'' she complained.

''Really?'' he murmured, his tone purring with satisfaction. She really had a great ass, toned and feminine and perfectly sized for his palms.

Bottom up in the air, her soft curves enticed him to do some additional exploring. At his touch, her thighs immediately parted and she sighed.

"Ohh. Ahh. You knew...all along that...I couldn't reach."

"I couldn't resist the view from such a delicious angle," he admitted.

"You realize I'm dangling here? That all the blood is rushing to my head."

"Let's see what we can do about that," he suggested, his savory thoughts turning wicked as pure delight shimmied through his veins.

The taut flesh of her bottom taunted him with a peek at golden curls between her parted thighs. The temptation proved too much for him and he dipped his fingers into her receptive warmth.

Greeted by her soft moan of approval, he explored the soft insides of her thighs, the gentle arch of her back, and everything between. The tiny oohs and aahs in the back of her throat deepened into soft moans of pleasure. Squirming beneath his touch, she lifted her hips provocatively.

Leaning forward, he dipped his head and took several sharp nips at her buttocks. His fingers fluttered in her core, fueling her blaze with a combination of soft caresses and love bites just hard enough to cause her to realize that he held her at his mercy, strung out on the razor's edge of need, balanced between wanting and satisfaction.

"I think you can reach that condom if you wriggle over the edge just a little more."

Her arms waved wildly toward the condom still out of reach, her hair in an upside-down halo around her head. "I'll...fall," she protested.

"Not a chance," he assured her, his voice deep with a stinging desire that he could barely contain.

She scooted out farther while he kept one hand on

her thighs to steady her and the other continued to delve into her core. As she stretched, her muscles tightened, creating the most interesting sensation around his fingers.

"Got it." The triumph in her tone was muffled with need. And then she wriggled away from him, denying him the pleasure of touching her.

She turned around until she faced him once again and waved the packet under his nose. Her eyes sparkled with a hint of devilry. "I'm going to enjoy putting this on you."

She reached for his balls that were already tight with his excitement and so sensitive that just the slightest caress threatened to set him off. He breathed deeply, willing himself to wait, to maintain control.

But as she cupped him and rolled him in her palm, she appeared bent on taunting him. He let her have her moment of fun until he could stand the sweet abuse no longer.

"If you don't put that condom on soon...there will be no need for it at all," he warned her.

The blue in her eyes mirrored the sky as she tilted her head to the side in speculation. "I'm betting you can last longer."

10

TONI HAD LONG SINCE passed the point where she thought before she spoke. Being naked tended to make her lose her inhibitions, and she and Grey had been naked together for hours. With the morning sun rising in the east and creating a fine sheen of perspiration on their warming flesh, the brilliant sky above and the soft bounce of the trampoline beneath them, she spoke with a boldness that made her feel very free, very alive, and more happy than she'd been in many months.

As she toyed with Grey's softness between her fingers, she appreciated that the man knew how to both give and receive, lead and follow. Ego didn't rule him. Pleasure did. And stroking the smooth flesh of his erection, watching him fight against squirming, had her on a power trip that inflamed her need to be with him.

She chuckled softly, languidly, flicked her thumb around the wide head of his sex, took satisfaction in his low moan. "I never knew paybacks could be so much fun."

He spoke between gritted teeth, his tone a purred warning. "You're going to spoil the fun if you…"

"If I?" she pressed, then bent over and placed the tip of her tongue along his sensitive ridge.

He sucked in air as if his life depended on it. Tiny beads of sweat popped out along his chest. And beneath her tongue, he surged between her lips.

"Enough." He pulled away with a gasp and breathed deeply for several moments, while she appreciated the clean lines of his body. Built like an athlete in his prime, with long, lean muscles that didn't bulk up, he reminded her of a fine sculpture that she'd seen in the Eastman Gallery. Nostrils flaring, the pulse in his neck galloping, his eyes bold and wild, he held himself completely motionless, exhibiting the ultimate control.

Locking her gaze to his, ignoring the shimmer of heat nestling in her belly and shooting deeper into her core, she tore open the condom packet. Slowly, gently, she rolled the protection over him, wishing they could be skin to skin, but unwilling to take any additional chances. Judging by the passion simmering through her, she was already risking far more than she'd bargained for.

She'd missed having passion in her life, but not this feeling of perpetual instability, of questioning each phase of what happened next. She felt as if she'd stepped out of a perfectly good airplane at twenty thousand feet. Now free-falling, she wondered if her parachute would open. The ride down might be the most rewarding of her life—if the landing didn't kill her.

She told herself to be strong. Some risks were worth taking.

She told herself she'd wanted more passion in her life. And now that she was getting it, she would never forgive herself if she backed away.

The more she enjoyed Grey's company, the higher the stakes became. She could no longer think of their weekend as a fling to relax and have a little fun. Not with the electricity continually arcing between them. Not when she feared being zapped by his magnetism.

His eyes compelled her hands to move over him, sheathing him in protection. And then like a racehorse sprinting from the gate, he shot toward her, his shoulders tumbling her onto her back. The soft mat of the trampoline cushioned her bottom as she rolled. The trampoline's springs squeaked. Her legs parted or Grey's knees opened her wider, she didn't know which. She only knew that he'd plunged into her, filling her with heat, again giving her that part of himself that she craved so much.

She hadn't counted on the bounce of the trampoline countering his thrusting hips. For his every action, there was an equal and opposite reaction. The deeper he drove into her, the higher her hips lifted, bouncing against his pelvis, flesh to flesh, creating the most electrifying friction. Every nerve sizzled and stretched.

Then he changed the angle of penetration, running the hard length of himself against her clit. There was no more teasing. No more subtlety. Just heat. Friction. And sensations that caused every muscle to draw tight in anticipation of release.

With his hands on either side of her head, his face above hers framed by the blue sky, the world seemed too bright, too radiant, too full of sensations to abide.

Closing her eyes, she concentrated on him. His heated breath fanning her ear. His hard chest, with crisp swells of hair, brushing against her responsive breasts. His straining cock rubbing her most sensitive places until her back bowed and her breath came in hot, hard gulps.

"You feel…terrific," she told him.

"I aim to please."

"I'd say your aim is a bull's-eye…just…about… perfect." She clutched his back, tried not to dig her fingernails into the fluid muscles that corded and bunched with his efforts.

In truth, he was perfect. Perfectly male. A perfect lover, made up of super-coordinated muscle and bone, driven by the expertise of his knowledge and free-wheeling passion.

She wrapped her legs around his waist, used the give in the trampoline's matting to achieve the optimum momentum. When he dipped his head to kiss her, his breath sweetly mixing with hers, their tongues mimicking his seduction, she plunged over the edge, her muscles spasming, clenching around him, taking him with her.

For long, wonderful moments, her senses spun out of control and she anticipated a soft comfy landing. But he reached between their bodies, his fingers finding the center of those sensations, extending the spasms, drawing out the pleasure until her mind went numb. She came again, the next orgasm spilling over her before the last had receded, the gratification so intense, she quivered from the aftershocks.

Startled by the intensity, she opened her eyes to find him staring at her face in joy and wonder. He collapsed on top of her, rolled so she ended up on top.

"Thank you," he murmured in her ear, his heartbeat fast and furious against hers. "You are one hot lady."

"You make me hot," she admitted, wondering when she'd ever felt this sated and relaxed.

She could lie here all day with him as if she hadn't a care in the world, except how long he'd take to recuperate so they could make love again. Experimentally, she tensed those muscles that held him inside her and found him still hard, wonderfully still ready.

Not one to question such a marvelous gift, now on

top, she slowly began to move her hips, upward, then downward. The extra give from the trampoline took a little getting used to, but the padding cushioned her knees and the spring made movement easier. But Grey's surprised and pleased expression egged her on.

With him under her and on his back, his hands were free to roam over her. He skimmed his fingers over her breasts, allowing his thumbs to settle on her nipples, rekindling the blaze and filling her with more fire. She wanted to make this as good for him as he had for her, but when his hands dipped between her thighs, her hips seemed to increase the tempo of their own accord.

She tried to hold back and wait for him, but her body, so sensitized to his touch, refused to cooperate. She lost track of time. She lost track of the ocean waves lapping the seawall and the sun shining down on them. The entire world narrowed to just the two of them. One man and one woman who fit together as if they'd been fashioned by a master sculptor, two pieces of the same whole.

When she climaxed again, she had to swallow back a scream. And, afterward, as they both caught their breaths and finally separated, she felt complete. Sated.

As glistening perspiration dried on her indulged flesh and he removed the condom, she closed her eyes again, thinking herself ready for a nap. However, Grey had other ideas. He tugged her by the hand and she opened her eyes as he helped her down from the trampoline.

"How about a dip in the pool?" he asked.

Before she could even answer, he pulled her in. The cool water on her hot skin invigorated and renewed her energy, but what pleased her more was that he never released her hand. They surfaced together and his gentle kiss touched her deeply.

She'd wanted their time together to keep progressing, and he'd done his best to comply with her wishes, opening up to her in ways she hadn't expected, in ways both large and small, and stirring emotions in her that gleamed as bright and shiny and promising as a newly minted copper penny. She liked the side of Grey that he allowed her to see but she couldn't help wondering about the part of himself he had yet to share. His reluctance to talk about himself added to his mystique but the times when he did open up became all the more precious.

They spent the rest of the day swimming, making love and napping. By the time he flew them back to New Orleans in the helicopter, she knew she was in deep trouble. Somehow her search for passion had turned into something more. Something she didn't want to name. Something that scared her right down to her toes.

She'd fallen in love.

A DAY LATER, MONDAY, Zane still hadn't put Toni from his mind. Holding to their bargain, since returning from the island, he'd written stories about their weekend in his column "Hot Scoops" and, just as he had predicted, sales had risen. Newsstands had sold out the recent editions. If business stayed this good, he wouldn't have to lay off anyone. However, every time he turned around, someone was mentioning her to him. His photographers wanted visuals of them together. The other newspapers kept phoning for interviews, which he not only refused but found annoying, and he had twenty party invitations on his desk. A television reporter from *Entertainment Tonight* had called, wanting to do a follow-up, but he'd declined all the offers.

This scoop could pull the paper out of the red, but money wasn't the deciding factor. He didn't want anyone else writing about Toni Maxwell.

Despite keeping to Grey's hectic schedule, thoughts of Toni had intruded into Zane's thoughts in the most unlikely and intrusive of ways. During an advertising meeting, he'd looked at pictures of models for their new ad campaign, but all he could see was Toni's golden skin, her blond hair and her marvelous eyes regarding him with a combination of sensual heat and invitation.

And when Stephen had insisted they review production costs, Zane's mind had glazed over, images invaded his thoughts of their romp in the pool, her frolicking grin and her splashing him as they'd played tag, then made love one last time on the beach.

Stephen peered over the conference table at Zane. "You know, there's an angle you might want to publish in 'Hot Scoops' that you haven't touched upon yet."

Zane peered at Grey's aide through the clear glasses that his brother always wore while reading paperwork. "What?"

Stephen tossed an article toward Zane. "Last week, Toni Maxwell and Senator Birdstrum were engaged."

"Senator Birdstrum?" His pulse tripped. Even though he didn't quite believe the gossip, he knew it was probably true. Zane read the article where the senator had announced his engagement. "Toni's name isn't mentioned."

Stephen's eyes glinted with either amusement or smugness that he'd out-scooped his boss. "Nevertheless, I have it on good authority that the senator bought her a ring and delivered it to her home."

Senator Birdstrum? While Toni hadn't revealed to him the name of her suitor, Zane realized that Stephen could very well be correct. Birdstrum had a clean reputation, if one discounted the rumors of his ties to certain ruthless elements in the city. For years the *Louisiana Daily Herald* had reported Birdstrum's unsavory contacts to the public, but they had never caught any hard dirt on the good senator. Nothing that would shock a jaded community like New Orleans.

And he was certainly a man who didn't take no for an answer. No wonder Toni wanted the senator to back out of his proposal. The influential senator could be vindictive when crossed.

"You know Toni Maxwell and the senator might be working together to sabotage the paper," Stephen suggested slowly.

Zane didn't want to believe it. When he'd first met Toni he'd been suspicious of her motives, but after he'd gotten to know her, he couldn't believe her guilty of sabotage and had made excuses for her. He'd allowed his feelings to overpower his logic. But now, he was forced to face facts. And the fact that she'd hidden her connection to the senator couldn't be ignored. As much as he hated to admit his disappointment in her, he had to look reality in the eye. The senator was an enemy of his newspaper and Toni had deliberately hidden her association with the man from Zane.

Zane didn't want to admit to Stephen that Toni hadn't told him about her connection to the senator, but that seemed pointless since Stephen already knew by his reaction a moment ago.

Zane frowned at Stephen. "The senator never gets his hands dirty."

"He doesn't have to. His future bride could be doing

his messy work for him, distracting you while he sends in troublemakers.''

''I hardly think that even the senator would stoop to having his bride sleep with me in order to bring down the paper,'' Zane hotly defended Toni, but doubts lingered. Why hadn't she mentioned the senator's name when she'd come clean? He should have asked, but had refrained, thinking the man's name unimportant.

''You're probably right,'' Stephen agreed.

The connection between Toni and Birdstrum had set Zane's jaw on edge. He hadn't planned to see her again for several reasons. She was a woman who wouldn't be satisfied unless their relationship progressed. Sex by and of itself wasn't enough for her. She had wanted to get serious; he hadn't. But he hadn't wanted to hurt her, either.

On the other hand, when around her, he had trouble thinking of anything else but sex. Together, they'd been electric. Well matched in passion and stamina. He'd repeatedly told himself that he wouldn't call her. It was over. Done. He'd written his last ''Hot Scoops'' column. He didn't want to be tied to a woman—not any, even Toni. And he was determined to let her go before he hurt her or he got in over his head. However, now he felt as if he was drowning and fighting to keep his head above water.

His first instinct was to call her and ask her why she'd withheld vital information from him. Yet, he hesitated.

Seeing her again would make him want her again. He needed to sever all connections.

Get a grip.

He was supposed to be a newspaperman. He had to get the job done. Perhaps he could send reporters to do the investigative work. That would certainly protect him from falling for her Miss Innocent act again. But he also knew he was best suited for the job since she was more likely to open up to him than a stranger.

He had to stay close to her for the sake of the newspaper. But what would she do to his sanity?

MUCH TO TONI'S SURPRISE, her sisters hadn't grilled her the moment she'd walked in the door late Sunday night. And though she'd gotten a great night's rest, she stalled at her closet, staring blindly at her clothes, trying to put the weekend in perspective. What exactly had happened between her and Grey on the island?

The way their fantasy weekend had ended provided no obvious clues. Grey had dropped her off at her house without saying one word about seeing her again. To his credit, he must have been even more exhausted than she since she'd at least napped during the chopper ride back to the city.

She wished she could relegate Grey Masterson and her weekend with him to simply a fling. Sure, the sex had been better than terrific. She'd learned things about her body she'd never known. Her weekend had gotten her exactly what she'd wanted. Passion. Publicity. She should be content, yet things with Grey felt somehow unfinished, up in the air.

The conversation had occasionally turned personal and Grey had listened to anything she'd cared to say. But he'd revealed little about himself. And she was puzzled by it. The man she'd come to know on the island seemed so unlike the man Lane Morrow had described in the book that they could have been alter egos. Morrow had described a man who always looked forward and planned for the future. But the Grey Toni knew lived in the moment.

She supposed different women could bring out different sides of a man's personality. But why had Lane Morrow sensed Grey's need for stability when Toni could have sworn he enjoyed chaos?

Troubled, deep in thought, she was relieved to have the kitchen to herself. Today was Bobby's day to sleep in late and come into the shop at noon. Jude had school and Mickey...

Where was Mickey? Toni poured a glass of fresh-squeezed orange juice and retrieved the morning paper. Grey must have written the column after they returned Sunday evening to make this morning's paper. "Hot Scoops" stared at her from the front page but she didn't read it.

Instead, she pressed the blinking red light on the answering machine and played back the messages. As several reporters requested interviews, she wondered if getting an unlisted number might be wise. Senator Birdstrum had called twice and her mother once. Two calls were for Mickey and Toni conscientiously wrote them down and left the paper hanging on the refrigerator by a magnet.

With her feelings uncertain and raw, she sipped the orange juice and wondered if she should call her mom. But what could she say to her? That she'd deliberately created a scandal to chase off Senator Birdstrum? Somehow she didn't think that would go over well. And she felt too fragile to put up with the hassle of explaining.

Best to simply go to Feminine Touch and open the doors. Let her normal routine settle her. So she got herself together and set off for work.

Within two blocks of her walk to Feminine Touch, Toni knew something was wrong. While the French Quarter was always unpredictable, filled with everything from tour guides that sold ghost and vampire tours, to horse-drawn carriages ridden by tourists, panhandlers and upscale shoppers, the press didn't make a habit of camping outside her shop, actually blocking the street traffic.

When she saw the *Hard Copy* van, she almost turned and ran the other way. But along with the reporters was a group of upscale shoppers who she couldn't bring herself to disappoint. Ignoring the microphones shoved in her face, walking on shaking legs past the flashing bulbs from photographers, Toni unlocked her front door and entered her shop.

For one moment, she let the familiar, soothing decor calm her frazzled nerves. Rack after rack of her designs in myriad colors. Shoes, hats and purses to accessorize with. The scent of new fabrics, the sheen of the freshly waxed floor and the glint of the polished glass candy dish, filled with lagniappe—the French custom of giving a little back to the customer after they made a purchase—usually all these served to calm her.

And then the shoppers and reporters rushed into the store. The phone kept ringing and Bobby came out of the back room to the front to answer it. Toni has assumed her sister would take her normal day off, but, apparently, she'd anticipated problems and had shown up early. Toni gave her a quick hug, grateful for her presence. Dressed in pink jeans and tube top, with her long dangling earrings and deep southern smile, Bobby was in her element. Nothing seemed to faze her as she spoke on the phone and racked up sales and sweet-talked the customers.

With the store in good hands, Toni dealt with the press and answered every question with a "no comment." She'd never expected her little scandal to get national coverage. The media attention had gotten way out of control, just like her feelings for Grey. Heartily wishing the paparazzi would leave, she did her best to ignore them, but it did no good.

The low murmur of activity in her store suddenly reached a crescendo. She looked up as the door opened. Senator Birdstrum walked in, followed by his aides.

Oh God.

Senator Birdstrum. There was no mistaking his blond hair that had just recently started to recede over his wide forehead and his startlingly piercing eyes that glinted from his deeply tanned face. His eyes focused on her.

Damn.

She swallowed hard, and saw right through his wide smile to the strain beneath. He greeted her shoppers but his handshakes seemed forced. Flashbulbs popped in his face as the reporters clamored for a statement.

At the attention, he posed, preened.

What in Hades was he doing here?

She'd never expected him to show up without an appointment. Unannounced. In front of the press.

Head high, Birdstrum marched toward Toni. She wished the floor would open under her feet and deposit her in another universe. But she couldn't be that lucky.

When he swept her into his arms, he ignored her gasp of astonishment. Before she could say a word, his mouth covered hers with a kiss. A dry kiss that froze her blood to ice. Anger chilled her and she placed her palms on his shoulders to shove him back. But he was as strong as a wrestler, and she couldn't budge him.

However, the longer he held her, the more the flashbulbs popped, until her rage froze to a solid block of ice. Just what the hell did he think he was doing? Coming in here as if he owned the place and kissing her in front of...the entire world. She wasn't going to just make the New Orleans papers, but national television news.

It would serve him right if she vomited all over him. Where was her loss of control when she needed it? Her mouth was dry and her muscles had gone rigid. She might as well have been made of stone.

The kiss probably lasted less than two horrible seconds, but seemed endless. Nothing like Grey's, who could heat her from lips to toes in a nanosecond. And when the senator finally released her mouth, she found that he'd ushered her into the private sewing room in the back of her store.

Too angry to calm herself before she spoke, she practically snarled at him. "Just what in hell do you think you are doing?"

He spoke mildly. "I've come to see my fiancée."

"We are not engaged. I sent back your ring."

He waved his hand in the air. "A mere technicality."

She regrouped and tried again. "Haven't you been reading the papers? You don't want to have your name associated with mine."

"But I do."

He sounded so pleased with himself that she wanted to throw her cutting shears at him. Instead, she thanked her lucky stars that her sister had come in today and had the good sense to keep the reporters up front and out of earshot.

Birdstrum grinned. "I came to tell you the good news in person."

"What news?"

"I just hired your father. He's moving to Washington immediately. He wanted to call but I told him I preferred to tell you in person."

Birdstrum had hired her father. The shards of frozen blood in her veins shattered into a thousand sharp pieces. No doubt the senator figured he now had more control over her than ever. But no way would she agree to marry him. The senator could hire and fire his employees, including her father, but he had no hold on her except that which she allowed him. And Toni knew that her father wouldn't want her to destroy her future to further his career. Still, she backpedaled slowly. Maybe there was a way to save this situation.

Toni tried to regroup and spoke again. "Politicians abhor scandals. Having your name associated with me will ruin your reputation."

"Not quite." He shot a grin at her that never reached his eyes. "According to the pollsters, my image is too conservative. So having my name coupled with yours may help me win the upcoming election."

"Doesn't it bother you that I spent the weekend with Grey Masterson?"

He shrugged. "I figure you're entitled to your friends and I'm entitled to mine. But after we get married, we'll have to keep our extracurricular activities off the front page."

He'd spoken so reasonably that her fingers itched to slap him. His view of marriage and infidelity left her numb. Sickened. And sorry for a man who would probably never stand a chance at happiness.

She would never agree with the senator's calculated

viewpoints. Even if Grey broke her heart, just having experienced passion was better than the senator's mercenary logic. At least she'd tried to live, had opened herself to the possibility of love and she was proud of herself for having the courage to have tried—even if she failed.

Here she thought her own behavior outlandish, but the senator's plan for their future was frighteningly outrageous. Not only didn't she want this man, she wasn't going to let him anywhere near sweet, naive Bobby.

Just when she thought matters couldn't possibly get any worse, she heard another commotion at the front of her store. More flashbulbs. And reporters shouting. Reporters who knew too much about her private life.

"Mr. Masterson, did you spend the weekend on your private island with Toni Maxwell?"

She realized the reporters must have spoken to a helicopter mechanic or someone who had refueled the chopper. That the reporter was willing to go to such lengths shook her. By creating this scandal, she'd given up her privacy.

They started shouting questions at her in the back room.

"Are you engaged to the senator, ma'am?"

"Are you involved in a ménage à trois?"

11

ZANE FIGURED THAT, RIGHT about now, Grey would have blown his cool. Being publicly outed by Lane Morrow's book had driven him to take a much-needed vacation. Grey took life seriously. Even when Grey had a fling, it meant something to him. Grey didn't do light and easy.

But even the laid-back Zane had to hide his annoyance with the woman who had so generously shared her body with him over the weekend. The woman who had played him for a fool. Even after Stephen had told him about her connection to the senator, even after Zane had read the article, he'd given her the benefit of the doubt.

That Grey had made a powerful enemy of the senator didn't surprise Zane. With their politics diametrically opposed, Grey had considered it his job to portray the politician in the worst light. And a powerful man like the senator wouldn't take kindly to criticism. However, Zane hadn't expected the man to use such underhanded tactics, or for Toni to go along with him.

He still had trouble believing it. But there were so many coincidences that not even he could keep making excuses for her. She'd been posing in her gorilla suit, distracting Grey when someone had poured oil into the ink and ruined the run. She'd been with him at Club Carnal when someone had poured sand into the fuel tanks and sabotaged the trucks. She'd had access to the computers right before the headlines had been almost disastrously changed. And now she'd hidden her connection to the senator.

It was time Zane faced the hard facts. Even if he didn't want to.

He'd come over to Feminine Touch to ask her for an explanation in person, only to find the press hovering in the front room like vultures. When he didn't see Toni, he headed straight to the back to find her standing much too close to Birdstrum, who didn't look the least bit upset by Zane's sudden appearance. In fact, the senator was practically gloating, his politician's phony grin plastered on his face, his hand outstretched.

As if Zane would shake it.

Birdstrum withdrew his hand, still not perturbed by Zane's rejection. "Keep up the good work, Masterson."

And then the SOB walked out the back door and slithered into a waiting car with tinted windows. Avoiding the press. Leaving Toni alone to sink or swim in the tide of Zane's fury and the press's dirty pool of curiosity.

To add to his confusion, Birdstrum was leaving Toni high and dry. It shouldn't irk him so, but it did. To her credit, Toni appeared relieved at the slimeball's disappearance. Then she turned, cheeks pale, eyes wide, hands trembling, nevertheless squaring her shoulders and lifting her chin to face him.

Zane thought she'd never looked so strong or more vulnerable and had to restrain himself from taking her into his arms. She'd betrayed him—sort of. At the least, lied to him, by omission. Of course, he could hardly hold that against her since he'd done the same. Toni didn't even know his first name.

Still, his motive for deception was to catch the person trying to harm the family business. Her motive was probably to get away with a crime. Although Zane reminded himself that he still had no hard evidence against her, the circumstantial evidence was damning.

He couldn't afford to allow his feelings to get in the way of business. Not this time. Still, he stalled, taking out the nonprescription glasses and settling them on his nose. "Why didn't you tell me Senator Birdstrum's your fiancé?"

"I already told you that he's not." She fisted her hands on her hips. "What is it about testosterone that gives men selective hearing?"

"I can't hear what *you* haven't bothered to explain. Why didn't you tell me that Birdstrum was the one?"

"He was none of your business."

"He's the reason you sought me out," he countered. "He's the reason you wanted to create a scandal."

"If you must know…I feared you'd write his name in the paper and ruin his reputation."

"You didn't trust me?"

"Why should I? We've just met."

Most likely she wanted to hide her complicity in sabotage. With her on the inside to tell the senator his every move, the risk of their criminal activity being discovered went way down. He cocked a skeptical brow and folded his arms over his chest. "That was the only reason? You were concerned I'd ruin Birdstrum's reputation?"

"Bobby's always seemed infatuated by the senator. I didn't want to do anything that might inadvertently hurt my sister."

"How admirable." He didn't bother reining in his sarcasm.

She ignored his derision. "My primary concern was for my father. The senator just hired my father, a career move Dad's hankered to make for years. I didn't want to hurt his chances." She huffed in frustration. "And I don't know why I'm explaining myself to you. What are you doing here?" she asked. "Why did you come?"

He thought quickly. Would she want to see him anymore? She could no longer claim that a scandal would make the senator reject her. Not after he'd increased his ties to Toni's family by hiring her father. Not after he'd just overheard the idiot Birdstrum telling her that he thought a scandal would enhance his political reputation.

Perhaps the rumors about the man's sexual orientation were true. Birdstrum might be gay. It would explain his eagerness to capitalize on a scandal with a female. And even if he was a heterosexual, Toni's association with both men might put the rumors to rest.

On the surface, there was no reason for her to continue their relationship. Unless she was up to no good. She had no idea he thought she and the senator were responsible for the sabotage.

So what was he going to do about it? He needed time to think, to consider, to figure out what he wanted to say.

He shot her his most charming smile. "Come to dinner at my place tonight?"

While he waited for her answer, his mind went through possible scenarios. One of his investigative reporters had tracked down the missing security guard's new work address. He'd ask Toni to his place for uninterrupted conversation and dinner, then bring her with him to look up the guard. Would she or the guard slip up and admit to knowing one another?

She frowned at him, clearly undecided about his invitation. "Why didn't you just call before showing up here?"

He had no chance to respond before Bobby ducked her head into the back room, where she'd guarded them from the press and allowed them privacy. She looked from Toni to Zane and back at her sister. "The press is finally gone and I could use a little help out here."

"Bobby, this is Grey Masterson. Grey, my sister Bobby," Toni introduced them. Bobby blushed, nodded and ducked back through the curtain.

The interruption had saved Zane from answering Toni's question about why he hadn't called. He couldn't exactly explain that he wanted to look into her eyes to gauge her honesty, so before she recalled her question, he closed the distance between then and did what he'd been dying to do since he'd first laid eyes on her.

She wore some blue concoction that brought out the color of her eyes and emphasized her curves. With her hair braided and clipped back from her face, she looked different than he'd remembered from the island, more sophisticated.

Her spicy perfume wafted up to him before he claimed her lips. She responded by winding her arms around his neck and parting her lips, leaning into his hardness as if she'd spent the hours since she'd last seen him missing him.

He knew better. But his suspicions couldn't dull the sharp pull of desire that shot through him or prevent his immediate arousal. She tasted of tangy lip gloss, a hint of toothpaste and orange juice—all wholesome flavors. But there was nothing wholesome about his response to her kiss. Apparently his sexual libido didn't care that she might have colluded with the senator to ruin his family's newspaper.

However, he didn't let the lower half of his anatomy make all his decisions. He told himself he would keep her close—until he could prove her guilt. And if he also enjoyed her body, he would have no feelings of remorse. After all, she'd come to him. And he gave her as much pleasure as he received.

So what if she kissed like a dream? He needed answers. So what if he wanted to drag her into bed and show her that she was on the wrong side? He needed her to be straight with him. They needed to have a serious conversation. The problem was, of course, if she was guilty, he knew better than to expect her to admit it.

Was she treacherous? Dangerous? All the more so because she was good at feigning innocence?

Grey had been taken in by such a woman and Lane Morrow had made public the reputation he preferred to keep private. Luckily Zane had more experience with duplicities. And he never put his heart on the line.

He'd told her that his secretary would phone with an address and directions and then left before he questioned her right then and there. Now was not the time.

He told himself that the reason he needed privacy was for their conversation. That his physical reaction to Toni Maxwell had nothing to do with his need to be alone with her.

He would wine her and dine her, sweeten her up with dinner and then pepper her with the hard questions. If Zane had his way, by the time they spoke to the security guard, she would have admitted all her secrets and revealed her true intentions.

He couldn't wait.

"YOU'RE IN LOVE WITH HIM, aren't you?"

Mickey had stopped in at Feminine Touch to say hello before work. Jude had come in after her environmental class, and since Bobby hadn't left due to the heavy store traffic, her sisters had Toni cornered. They'd pitched in to help and after how hard they'd worked, Toni was feeling grateful that, once again, they'd been there for her.

With the publicity "Hot Scoops" had generated, she'd sold more clothes today than she normally did in a month. She'd already called her supplier to order more fabric and thread and placed an ad in the classified section of the paper looking for additional seamstresses. With the daily receipts counted and tallied for a bank deposit, the last customer long gone, all Toni wanted to do after her harrowing day was go home, kick off her shoes, soak under a hot shower and climb into bed. Being grilled by her sisters didn't enter into her picture of fun things to do.

"Him? Toni's in love with Senator Birdstrum?" Jude leaned over the counter to frown with confusion at Mickey, who stood by the window and straightened a gown in the display.

Bobby smoothed her pink tube top in front of a mirror, then spun around to face her sisters. "Senator Birdstrum is gay. Our sister is not in love with him."

"What?" Toni gaped at Bobby. Gay? But he'd asked her to marry him. Yet, she realized, his homosexuality would account for his coolness toward her.

His easy acceptance of another man in her life because he didn't care. The pieces fit.

Mickey picked a piece of lint off the gown in the window, then carefully pulled one of the deep velvet waiting chairs into the reception area and sat down. Ignoring the conversation about Birdstrum, Mickey wrinkled her forehead, clearly focused on her own thoughts. "Toni's in love with Masterson. Grey Masterson."

"Why can't she marry one man and take the other as a lover?" Jude said calmly, but Toni knew she didn't mean it.

"I don't want the senator," Toni said with exasperation.

"Which is good, because," Bobby plucked the pink barrette from her hair, threaded her fingers through her locks, the replaced the barrette and spoke to Jude, "the senator already has a lover."

"When did you find out the senator has a lover?" Mickey demanded of Bobby.

"I've known since I saw him kissing his chauffeur last week," Bobby admitted, digging into her purse.

"His chauffeur? His male chauffeur?" Mickey frowned. "And you didn't tell her?"

Bobby reapplied her pink lip gloss. "I liked her plan to create a scandal way too much to spoil her fun."

"You little devil," Jude breathed out. "Toni might never have forgiven you if she hadn't—"

"Fallen in love with Masterson?" Bobby's cheeks glowed with triumph as if she'd personally engineered the matchmaking.

"Toni could have been hurt," Jude protested.

"You should have told her." Mickey glared at

Bobby. "Toni thought you were infatuated with the senator."

Bobby's eyes glinted. "I know."

Jude looked from Bobby to Mickey and back. "She didn't want to marry a man you were interested in."

"Uh, you guys. You know I'm here, right?" Toni finally called out.

"I was never interested in the senator, only his tactics," Bobby admitted. "He's a master at keeping secrets from the public and at keeping his private life…private. We've all heard the rumors and never believed them. The man is a master strategist. And… I've been thinking about a career in politics."

Bobby? Toni's thoughts spun. When had she become so wrapped up in her work and her own personal life that she'd failed to recognize her sister's ambition? Although she'd never expected Bobby to work as a salesclerk for the rest of her life, she'd never had a clue about her sister's interest in politics. However, Bobby always seemed to get exactly what she wanted—in a cute, adorable, very pink way. If she ever hit Washington in her pink suit, those stodgy politicians wouldn't know what hit them.

Toni's lips turned into a grin of approval. "Bobby, hon, you'd make a great politician."

"I can see it now, Bobby Maxwell for President," Jude agreed.

"Yes, but we're talking about Toni's love life right now," Mickey bullheadedly brought the conversation back round to where she'd started it.

Somehow, Toni had known she wouldn't get off so easily.

Jude leaned her elbow onto the counter and propped

her chin into her hand. "Tell us about your weekend, Toni."

"Yes, do," Bobby agreed.

"Was the wildlife as spectacular as—"

"The only wild life I want to hear about," Mickey interrupted, "is our sister's."

Making love with Grey had been wild. First on the horse, then on the trampoline and later on the beach. But how did Mickey know? Did Toni's satisfaction show on her face? Could her sister see into her dreamy eyes and read her salacious thoughts? Could her sister tell how aware Toni was of her own body, that Grey had teased every inch of her? Her breasts, still tender, hardened at the memory of Grey suckling them. The man had a wicked tongue and she couldn't wait for their next encounter. At least Birdstrum's arrival this morning hadn't caused Grey to back away, but then Grey seemed to adore challenges—which didn't exactly jive with her image of a conservative businessman.

In fact, she'd expected Grey to hide his playful sexual nature, but he'd been much more open than even Lane Morrow's book had led her to believe. She'd thought business would be his life. But he'd so easily delegated responsibilities that he hadn't appeared to be the hardheaded, driven executive that she'd come to expect after reading Lane Morrow's book. Only once had Grey seemed surprised by her behavior and acted conservatively and that had been during their first encounter in his office when she'd danced in wearing her gorilla suit. But, ever since, he'd been a different man. Caught up in his whirlwind personality, she hadn't had time to ponder or reflect. And now, from the silent treatment her sisters were now giving her, they clearly expected her to give up her feelings.

But some things shouldn't be shared. Her memories of Grey on the island were private. "I'm not ready to talk yet. And I don't have time, either," she added before any of them could protest. "Grey asked me to dinner tonight."

"And she said yes," Bobby exclaimed with satisfaction. "On a weeknight."

Jude grinned. "With work tomorrow?"

"Shut up," Toni ordered affectionately, then headed toward a clothing rack. "Unless you all have something constructive to say, I don't want to hear it."

Even Mickey's eyes twinkled with glee. "The French lingerie you ordered last spring arrived this afternoon while you were waiting on Ms. Carson. Perhaps you might want to sample some of your new stock?"

Ms. Carson had always been one of Feminine Touch's best customers. A celebrity in her own right, a famous comedienne who worked the late-night show at the riverfront casino, she'd maxed out her credit card, complaining that with Feminine Touch's new celebrity, the stock was already thinning. Mickey had assured Ms. Carson that she'd always have enough stock, even if she had to spend her nights sewing her fingers to the bone. Ms. Carson had chuckled and told her that nights in New Orleans were for partying and love.

The late-afternoon hours had turned even more hectic and Toni had totally forgotten the new shipment until Mickey had mentioned it. Sinfully sexy French lingerie might be just what she needed to perk up her spirits. She didn't even feel tired anymore and practically floated her way into the back room.

With her sisters' help, they opened the cartons and unpacked the expensive goodies from Aubade, Chantal Thomas, Alternate Plaisir, and pure silk handmade lingerie from De Pledge. After her long day, the idea of showering then pampering herself in luxurious elegance, indulging in the crème de la crème of lingerie, appealed to her.

"Oh my," Bobby squealed at a soft, barely pink baby doll in a floral design with delicate underwire cups.

Toni handed it to her. "It's yours."

Bobby took one look at the price on the itemized inventory and shook her head. "I couldn't."

"You can and you will," Toni insisted.

When Jude seemed partial to a soft beige lace bustier with an attached sheer skirt lavishly trimmed with the finest lace ruffles, Toni gave it to her. Aware that Mickey would never knowingly reveal her preference, Toni watched her eyes carefully. And when her younger sister studiously ignored a classic-style button-front tailored charmeuse and chiffon shadow-stripe sleepshirt, Toni plucked it from the pile and handed it over, enjoying the feel of the expensive and beautiful material.

Mickey shook her head. "I appreciate the thought, really. But keep it for inventory—I'll never wear it."

"Mickey, you may not admit to a softer side, but you're just as romantic as the rest of us." Toni shooed her away. "You just haven't found the right man yet."

Mickey looked over her shoulder and raised an inquiring brow. "And you have?"

She tossed aside delicate silk stockings to dig through the pile for exactly the right lingerie. "I know. I know. It seems like madness. But I'm in love."

"And does he return your feelings?" her sister asked wisely.

"He doesn't have a clue." She sighed, plucking a sheer demi-bra and matching panties from the bottom of the box. "The challenge will be getting him to see me not just as a lover but as someone he needs in his life for the long-term."

"And if he doesn't see the light?" Mickey's voice deepened in concern.

Her heart skittered and slid with worry that Grey might never change, but she held her sister's gaze. "A man who doesn't want me isn't worth having."

ZANE HAD A CHEF FROM one of the best New Orleans restaurants cook them a meal and deliver it by taxi to Grey's apartment. He showered as delicious scents of garlic and peppers scented the air in the kitchen. He'd set the table with Grey's fine china and had a bottle of wine on ice. Soft music, instrumental, played out of surround-sound speakers, and he'd pulled the drapes closed to give the glass room a feeling of intimacy.

Whistling as he soaped his hair and rinsed in the shower, Zane contemplated his evening. Eager to see Toni again, eager to confront her with his suspicions, he was ready to forgive her to find out the truth.

Senator Birdstrum could wield powerful strings. Toni might have been used without her knowledge. Maybe blackmailed. Zane wouldn't put anything past the ambitious senator.

He'd just padded out of the shower when the doorbell rang. Slinging a towel around his hips, he padded barefoot to the front door. He opened it to Toni's smiling face, and his breath hitched in his chest.

She was wearing one of those provocative slip

dresses, a deep purple gown with tiny, wispy straps to hold it up. The fabric clung to her curves, molded to her hips all the way down to her matching spiked heels. He didn't know how she could possibly walk, until he noted the long, lethal slit at the thigh that caused him to release a low whistle of appreciation.

"Wow." He stepped back, holding the door wide, breathing in the scent of her jasmine perfume as she entered.

She didn't so much as flicker one long eyelash at his state of undress. Although she had seen his bare chest before, he couldn't help but feel a tad miffed when she took more interest in the room than in his very wet, very naked flesh.

Grey had hired some designer to decorate, and her inquisitive gaze skimmed over the leather couches, the light oak tables, with their art deco lamps, to the eclectic art collection on the walls. Although Grey was partial to renaissance nudes in gold frames, he also collected Andy Warhol and Picasso.

"What do you think?" he asked.

"It's nice."

"Nice is such a bland word."

Her gaze settled on a display shelf, the only objects in the room that actually belonged to Zane. He'd taken the collection, which he'd begun many years ago, with him because he hadn't wanted Grey to see them. As if drawn to his collection, she strolled toward the shelf. "That, that looks like..."

"Yes?"

"Glass dildos?" Her eyes lit with amusement and curiosity.

"They're made of handblown glass." He plucked one of them from the shelf and handed it to her. Although he possessed pieces of erotic jewelry that came from his friend Reina Price, she didn't work in glass. He'd purchased the pieces from Shamar, another artist displayed at Reina's gallery.

"It's heavy. Smooth." She ran her fingers over the glass sculpture. Naturally, he couldn't help recalling when she'd done exactly the same thing to him. Only he hadn't been made of glass; he'd stiffened and swelled...and now he ached to do so again.

He reminded himself that he'd asked her here to talk. But it was odd how she'd automatically approached the only objects in the room that weren't Grey's. He hadn't wanted to leave his erotica collection behind. No telling what his brother would have thought of the objects. They had been crafted as carefully as any artistic sculpture, yet they were undeniably outrageous.

"The glass is fired at high temperatures to prevent any chance of breakage." Zane watched her fingers close over the base and he swallowed hard.

Down, boy.

She noted the towel tenting at his hips and smacked her lips, yet continued to fondle the dildo. "I'm suddenly feeling overdressed." She turned around and gave him her back. "Would you mind unzipping me?"

Mind? Of course he wouldn't mind. His plans for conversation were sinking faster than the *Titanic.*

He swept her hair from her shoulders with a delicate caress, his fingers tingling. Still, he made an attempt to keep to his original plan. "Don't you want to eat first? Aren't you hungry?"

"Unzip me, and then I'll let you decide exactly what you're hungry for."

He did as she asked, tugging down the zipper slowly, revealing the soft, smooth flesh of her back. Kissing each inch before he revealed the next. He'd fully intended to feed her dinner and talk to her about his suspicions, but that could wait.

He couldn't.

And then the microwave that had been heating the pasta dinged. "I should get that."

At his words, she shimmied her hips and the gown pooled at her feet. At first he thought she was nude. But then he saw the flesh-colored filmy lingerie. Suddenly he couldn't wait for her to turn around. She'd dressed to seduce him and the thought heated his blood.

She stepped out of her dress, carefully picked it up, then tossed it onto the couch. Slowly, very slowly, she turned around.

She was wearing a sinfully strapless bra that lifted her breasts, but left her nipples bared. And panties cut so high, they emphasized her slim hips and tight bottom.

He sucked in his breath. "The food can wait."

But immediately after he said the words, the oven timer dinged, signalling it was time to remove the garlic bread from the oven. Mouth watering, he backed into the kitchen. "There will be a fire if I don't at least take the bread out of the oven."

Step for step, she followed him, the glass dildo still in her hands. He swiped the dildo's mate from the shelf, an idea starting to form in his mind. She wanted to play, did she? Well, he hadn't given her all the particulars about his collection. However, he much preferred showing to telling.

"I'm good in the kitchen," he told her, keeping the joke to himself for now.

She licked her bottom lip provocatively. "I'm counting on it."

12

TONI HAD HOPED HER NEW lingerie would incite Grey's lust, but for a man so obviously ready to make love, he was acting oddly. He dashed around the kitchen, removing a tray from the oven, another from the microwave, then, instead of giving his attention to her, he removed a glass jar from a cabinet next to the sink, filled the jar with water and set it inside the microwave.

Finally, he leaned forward to kiss her, at the same time, he removed the glass dildo from her hands. Her back to the counter, she leaned against the edge for support, no longer caring about the sculpture, focusing her attention solely on Grey. He tasted like chicory, the thick coffee New Orleans made famous, and she realized he had a pot perking on the counter.

Behind her, she heard him open the fridge—no, make that the freezer, she amended as frigid air blew over her almost bared skin, causing her to shiver, raising goose bumps on her back, and making her nipples pucker. While she didn't mind him preventing their dinner from burning, she wished he'd stop fussing and put his hands on her.

She broke the kiss, irritated. "Will you stop with the cooking stuff and warm me up?"

"Yes, ma'am." His eyelids shuttered, hiding a gleam of amusement.

"It's no fun when you're more concerned with—"

His mouth swooped down over hers, stifling her complaint. His tongue insinuated itself between her lips, teasing, tasting and taunting. She sighed into him in appreciation.

This was more like it.

A kiss she could sink into and appreciate. A warm-up for what was to come. The man could kiss, she had to give him that. He seemed to know exactly how much pressure to apply and where to apply it, yet she sensed his thoughts weren't totally focused on her. How could they be, when he'd opened the cabinet behind her to remove a cruet of, she turned her head slightly...*olive oil?*

With his flesh still damp from the shower, rivulets of water from his wet hair dripping over the hard muscles of his neck, shoulders and chest, she considered lapping up every drop off his warm skin to distract him from his cooking activities. If she hadn't been so sure that he wanted her, she might have pulled back in a huff. But his hard sex brushing through the towel and against her hip clearly told her of his interest. An interest she intended to intensify.

The microwave dinged again. She started and muttered a curse. She could have sworn he'd smothered a chuckle. But when she fired her sharp gaze at him, he appeared the picture of innocence. From beneath eyelashes spiked with water droplets, he pinned her against the countertop between the microwave and the freezer.

"You aren't going to do more cooking, are you?" she complained.

At her impatient frown, his eyes twinkled with mirth. "If you must have me now, I'll set the delay on the timer."

"Make it a protracted delay," she urged.

He reached behind her to press a few buttons, but she paid no further attention. She was much more interested in removing the knotted towel from around his hips. Her fingers fumbled and she'd just succeeded, when the microwave timer dinged again.

"I could learn to hate that sound."

He reached inside, removed the glass jar. With her back to the microwave, she couldn't see what he was doing and paid no attention to the movements of his hands behind her back. Instead, she lapped up a trickle of water at his neck, pleased that his pulse was so erratic.

From a glance at his expression, he might appear unaffected by her seduction, but there could be no denying her effect on him or the fullness of his erection, which encouraged her—even if he did keep puttering with kitchen stuff.

Surely she was up to distracting him from a microwave and jars of water and olive oil. She used her tongue to follow the flow of water from his neck to his nipple, pleased when he sucked in his breath, displeased when he had the presence of mind to reset the microwave buttons.

When the damn thing dinged again, seemingly only five seconds later, she retaliated by taking his nipple between her teeth and biting down lightly. Holding him immobile, she spoke in a half mumble. "Don't move."

"But—"

She bit down just a little harder.

"Hey—"

With her free hand she reached between his legs and teased his balls. Still, he managed to hit the reset button on the microwave.

But if she'd needed more evidence of his arousal,

she now had it. He was drawn so tight that his legs quivered. Sensing he wouldn't try to move, she relaxed her teeth on his flesh and laved the nipple with soothing licks. Slowly, she rolled his flesh in her palm, stroking him where he was hard, caressing him where he was soft.

This time when the microwave dinged, he didn't move, just spoke between gritted teeth. "It's going to be payback time soon, lady."

"Mmm."

But she didn't have patience for his games right now. Not as she teased his flesh with her lips and tongue. Not when giving him pleasure brought her to a fever pitch of need.

She longed to have him inside her. And suddenly she recalled the condom in her purse, way across the kitchen in the living room. Damn.

Now that she had him just where she wanted him, she wasn't about to leave. He might decide to bake cookies or brownies. On the other hand, she wouldn't have unprotected sex. She might love the big lughead, but she wasn't ready to risk a pregnancy.

He must have sensed her hesitation. "Something wrong?"

Her gaze lifted to his, then to the towel she'd discarded on the floor. "I don't suppose you have a condom nearby?"

He opened a kitchen drawer so far the drawer came completely free of its hardware. Aluminum foil, Ziploc baggies and garbage twist ties fell to the floor. He tried the drawer on their other side. No luck. Instead, plastic lids and wooden spoons tumbled out of the drawer to the floor.

"There might be one over—"

She didn't ask why he had condoms in his kitchen drawers. She'd known from the start there'd been women before her and wouldn't hold his past against him.

"Way to go, bro," he muttered. Or that's what she thought he said.

"Huh?"

He held up a packet in triumph. "Ta-da. I told you I was good in the kitchen."

Pleased with his find, unwilling to ask for explanations, she tried to go back to exploring his body, but he hooked his thumbs into her panties and removed them, then he clasped her waist with his big hands and lifted her onto the kitchen counter. The sparkly white granite felt pleasantly cool against her bare buttocks.

"I'll do the honors." She reached for the condom, but he flipped it out of her reach.

"Not yet."

Very deliberately, he placed her arms behind her, palms down so she could comfortably support herself, then nudged her thighs wide. She expected him to come to her, not reach for the cruet of olive oil.

Then he opened the microwave. All along she'd thought he'd been heating water for dinner, but she'd been very mistaken. Behind her back where she couldn't see what he'd been doing, he'd placed the glass dildo in the heated water. And now he dribbled the olive oil over the glass sculpture with intense concentration.

As she figured out his intentions, her mouth went dry. "You want to…"

"Do you?"

She stared in fascination as he smoothed the oil over the glass until the dildo was thoroughly coated. As much as she'd wanted him inside her, she couldn't help her curiosity. And yet, she'd never done anything like this.

"We can stop anytime you like," he told her, testing the heat against the inside of his wrist. "I used a microwave thermometer. The glass is heated perfectly to one hundred and ten degrees."

He hid the glass sculpture between her parted thighs. Just close enough to sense the heat.

"I wanted *you* inside me."

"This will be double the thrill," he promised.

When she hesitated, he rubbed the slippery glass along her inner thigh, shooting a tingling sensation straight to her center. Making love with Grey would never be boring. He could be incredibly innovative, exciting, and she intended to more than keep up with him.

As if sensing her compliance, he drizzled more olive oil directly between her legs. Tiny, delicious trickles suddenly made it difficult for her to hold still.

Voice husky, she pleaded, "Touch me."

His eyes focused on her in appreciation, his nostrils flaring with each breath. He stood between her thighs like a man focused on a mission. Intense. Complex. His chin jutted with determination and his lips tightened as he held back his own need to give her pleasure.

Slowly, ever so carefully, he parted her aching flesh and rubbed the smooth glass against her. Sensations like she'd never known danced along her tender skin.

"Oh...my. I'm...so...hot."

"You certainly are."

Licking his bottom lip as if hungry to taste her, he suddenly shot her a wicked grin. A charming grin. A grin that eagerly awaited her reaction.

He slid the rounded tip of the heated glass into her. The warmth and pressure had her suddenly frantic to pump her hips.

"Hold still," he ordered as if reading her thoughts. "Talk to me. Tell me how you feel."

"Give me more," she demanded. "Hurry."

He moved slow and easy, his thumb flicking over her clit, while he inserted another warm inch.

She lifted her hips, tilting them, eager to take all the heat inside her at once. "More."

He gave her more, his thumb swirling, and then he leaned forward, taking her nipple into his mouth. His lips grazed the lace of the demi-bra she still wore and she arched into him, frantic with need. With his tongue licking a flame of pure sizzling energy at her breast, his fingers busily creating magic and the heat from the glass inside her, she was about to go off like a firecracker.

Her head was numb, as if all her blood had left and gone south. And when he began to move the dildo in and out, she tilted her head back and uttered a long, low moan. "I'm going to...I'm going to...explode."

"No, you aren't." His voice was tight. "Close your eyes and tell me that you are going to hold back."

She didn't hesitate to follow his demand. He opened the freezer again. "Maybe some cool air will slow down your burn."

But after she closed her eyes, all she could think about was that every cell in her body was about to erupt through the top of her head. A little cool air from the freezer wouldn't douse the flames.

"If you want me...to hang on, then...just stop for a second."

He paid no attention and she couldn't help wondering why he was urging her over the edge this way. Almost as if he had something to prove—to himself.

"Give me just one second."

Instead of relief, he moved his fingers faster between her legs, increasing the pressure and she bit her lip to contain a scream.

His voice stopped coaxing and commanded. "Not yet. Wait."

"I...don't think...I can."

Despite every effort to obey, her body wasn't listening. He'd set her blood on fire. She couldn't breathe. She couldn't wait another second.

And then just as she began to spasm, he pulled out the heat. And plunged in ice.

A crazy uproar of intense sensation shot her over the edge into blissful fire and ice. Hot and cold. And pure unadulterated release. She couldn't hold back a scream. Or the shudder that racked her with such pleasure she felt faint. Instinctively, she fell forward into his arms, her mind spinning, her body trembling. She lacked the strength to flex a muscle, lacked the willpower to attempt anything more than enjoy the exquisite pleasure he'd given her.

It took several long moments, maybe minutes, for her to regain just a semblance of her senses. He held her against his chest, cushioning her head under his chin.

"That was unbelievable...that switch from hot to cold," she finally said.

He chuckled. "That's why I positioned you between the microwave and the freezer."

And she'd been thinking he was cooking dinner. She should have guessed. When she tilted her head back to look up at him, satisfaction gleamed in his eyes.

Clearly he was pleased with his kitchen accomplishments, more pleased that she hadn't been able to hold back.

Even now she quivered with the aftereffects. The experience had boggled her mind and frazzled her senses, but what she really wanted right now was Grey. Grey's arms around her. Grey inside her.

"What?" he asked.

"It might be fun to do that again sometime but—"

"But—"

She craned her head, looking down a hallway. "Doesn't this apartment have a room more suited to lovemaking, perhaps one with a bed?"

OF COURSE HIS BROTHER had a bed, a king-size thousand-count cotton-sheeted four-poster bed with a gold quilted coverlet that Zane had swept to the thickly carpeted floor before he'd lowered Toni into the middle. They'd made love twice since, and he'd forgotten about his ruined plans. A man as satiated as he had no right to complain when his woman had taken care of him so well, so completely.

His woman? Just when had Zane started to think of her as his? He wanted to shove the alarming thought away. She had just slipped into his thoughts and arms so naturally that he hadn't had the chance, or the heart, to take even one step back.

But over the past several hours, one thing had become very clear to him. He wanted Toni in his life. He enjoyed her company way too much to let her activities come between them. Whatever she had done, they would undo. Whatever trouble she'd gotten herself into, he would help her get out.

He'd only been kidding himself earlier by telling

himself that he could let her go. He'd been in lust before and had found the attraction decreased in direct proportion to the amount of sex he engaged in. But with Toni, the more he had, the more he wanted.

He didn't just want her, he craved her. And not just her sultry body but her beautiful, creative and open mind.

And he wasn't going to give her up—even if she had helped sabotage the paper. She hadn't succeeded. No real harm had been done. In fact, thanks to her and his "Hot Scoops" column, the *Louisiana Daily Herald* was doing great. He was willing to let bygones be bygones.

With her wrapped in his arms, their breath mingling, their legs entwined, their arms around one another, he didn't want to let her go. In fact, he couldn't help thinking how great it might be to wake up in the morning and know the name of his bedmate *before* he opened his eyes.

He supposed he should figure out exactly what he wanted, but right now he didn't want to muster the energy or upset the equilibrium they'd established. Just because he wanted her again at this moment, didn't mean he'd feel the same way next week. Zane knew his strengths and his faults, which were sometimes one and the same. He tended to live for the next new toy—whether it be a better trampoline or helicopter—the next new city—whether it be Rio, Paris or Istanbul—or the next woman—whether she be blond, redhead or brunette. But, right now, he couldn't seem to get enough of Toni—a totally new experience.

His twin claimed he simply avoided commitment, but Zane knew he just liked to be different. The pattern had started when he and Grey had been children and parents, teachers and nannies had difficulty telling them apart. He'd wanted his own identity, forged his character by going his own way. If Grey zigged right, Zane zagged left. If Grey was the conservative businessman, Zane was the laid-back playboy. The lifestyle had suited him and eliminated all competition between the brothers.

Right now, Zane wanted the woman who slept in his arms. But for how long?

When his phone rang, Toni barely stirred. Zane reached over her and picked up the receiver. "Yes?"

"Sir, if you intend to arrive before the shift ends, we need to leave within fifteen minutes."

"Be down in a few minutes," Zane told the driver-bodyguard he'd hired for tonight's investigation. As he gazed at Toni deep in sleep, he hesitated to wake her. Perhaps he should go alone.

He'd intended to have answers from her long before now. Perhaps taking her with him would be better. He need not accuse her, but could simply watch her reactions to the guard. Zane hoped he knew her well enough by now to be able to tell if she was lying. And his heart tightened.

Regardless of her guilt or innocence, he needed to know the truth.

TONI APPRECIATED THAT Grey hadn't left her sleeping in his bed with a note to explain his absence. Instead, he'd told her about his intentions to question his former security guard and she'd volunteered to go with him.

However, when she'd seen the size of his "chauffeur" and glimpsed the gun holstered under the man's loose-fitting suit jacket, she'd had second thoughts. Settled in the plush back seat of his sedan, Toni fidgeted with her hemline. She wasn't exactly dressed to go skulking around back alleys and dark streets. Running in her spiked heels would likely break an ankle.

Grey wore a black turtleneck shirt, a dove-gray jacket and matching slacks with polished dress shoes. Elegant but comfortable, he appeared alert, yet relaxed.

She glanced from the driver to Grey. "You think the man we're going to meet is dangerous?"

"The driver's just a security precaution."

She didn't feel reassured. And while she wasn't sure if she expected Grey to protect her, she damn well knew he had no business putting her in jeopardy.

As the driver stopped before one the city's twenty-four-hour casinos, she relaxed a little. Under the bright lights, under security cameras that constantly monitored the gamblers, under a multitude of security, they should be quite safe.

She still must have had a puzzled look on her face because Grey explained, "Stiller took another job."

"Security?"

"Gambling. He runs a blackjack table."

"Don't these places do thorough background checks on their employees?"

"Stiller's clean. No criminal record. We checked him out before we hired him, too."

Inside, the casino was brightly lit and the dark red carpet cushioned her pointed heels. The nickel slots stood in rows closest to the front doors. And here gamblers wore everything from ten-year-old jeans and ratty shirts to designer apparel. Bells rang and lights on poles flashed every few minutes signalling a winner. However, the mood wasn't merry or frivolous. An elderly woman inserted coins with surprisingly agile fingers considering her hands looked painfully twisted from arthritis. She stared at the tumbling numbers and when they stopped and she lost, she tried again with a quiet desperation that squeezed Toni's heart. Even if the woman won, she'd no doubt feed her winnings right back into the hungry slot.

Too many of New Orleans's unfortunates ended up here. But gambling was good for the city, good for tourism and every restaurant owner and shopkeeper in the city knew that gambling increased their traffic and profits. As Toni walked side by side next to Grey, they passed blackjack and crap tables while the casino's employees plied customers with free drinks.

There were no windows to indicate if it was day or night. No clocks on the walls to tell that time had passed.

She shivered slightly. Toni had nothing against a fun night out, playing with money one could afford to lose. And she wasn't usually so judgmental. She suspected the dark cloud that had settled over her had nothing to do with their location but more with the man they were about to meet. Ever since Grey had awakened her, she'd been unable to shake the ominous feeling that weighed her down like a heavy cloak.

Already she missed being in his arms. Wanted to return to his big bed and forget about business. Until now, he'd been most considerate about keeping his newspaper responsibilities from interfering with their relationship, so now it seemed odd that he'd suggested coming here in the middle of the night.

Grey placed a casual arm around her shoulder. "Mr. Stiller works here but he's also a gambler himself, and not a very good one—although he's recently paid off a hefty sum of a very large debt."

"How did he pay off the debt?" she asked him,

appreciating any distractions from her previous thoughts. She tried to cheer herself with her newfound feelings for the man beside her.

She loved Grey. She loved the way he listened, really listened, when she talked. She loved the way he made love. She loved the way he made her feel about herself, as if she was extraordinary.

But despite the casino security, despite his arm over her shoulders, her wary instincts wouldn't calm. Being here with Grey simply didn't feel right.

Then a croupier nodded a greeting, "Evening, Mr. Masterson," and a barmaid handed them dry martinis, claiming it was his "usual," her friendly smile saying he could have much more than a drink. Toni realized that Grey frequented the casino more often than made her comfortable.

And she didn't know why. Grey could certainly afford to gamble. However, the activity seemed so out of character. She refused the drink but Grey kept his and sipped in seeming appreciation.

Grey spoke softly into her ear. "My source told me Mr. Stiller plays poker in one of the back rooms after he finishes his shift at the blackjack table."

"Your source?"

"I put out the word that I wanted to talk."

He put out the word? To whom?

She didn't have the opportunity to ask as the "chauffeur" rejoined them, his silent presence little comfort to her. Before she could think of another question, Grey swept her through an open doorway, his bodyguard following.

This room, filled with cigar smoke, mirrors and the ever-present bright lights, was just as red as the rest of the casino. Red carpet, red decorations, red-dressed waitresses. But the pace was a little less frenetic. Men and women, young and old, black and white, rich and poor, hunched over their cards in quiet concentration.

Without hesitation, Grey walked directly over to a short, overweight man with thinning black hair, leathered skin and pocked cheeks. At the sight of Grey and his bodyguard, Stiller threw in his hand, stood and tried to brush right past them.

Grey clasped the other man by the arm, halting him. "I'd like a word with you, Stiller."

"I don't work for your brother no more. Let me go. I've got nothing to say to you."

His brother? Stiller's words confused Toni. Stiller had worked for Grey's brother?

"You know me?" Grey asked, stiffening, and she thought his reaction odd.

"I've seen you around," Stiller admitted. "What of it?"

Grey set down his drink, mostly untouched, and lowered his voice, but the honed edge of pure threat under his gentlemanly southern speech couldn't be missed. "The *Daily Herald* is a family business. Or didn't you bother to learn that before you put sand in our trucks?"

"I didn't. I was...sick."

"And you're going to get a lot sicker if you don't cooperate."

Grey tugged the man through a doorway into another gaming room that was currently empty. Toni imagined the casino opened it during the high season of Mardi Gras. Right now she simply appreciated the smoke-free air, hoping it would clear her head. Grey was no longer acting like the Grey she knew and while she didn't expect him to turn violent, Stiller appeared to take his threat seriously. His former employee trembled and wouldn't look them in the eyes.

"You ain't got no right to threaten me," he mumbled.

"That wasn't a threat." Grey shoved the now sweating Stiller into a chair. "It was a promise."

Stiller's gaze went to the closed door as if contemplating making a run for freedom, but the bodyguard blocking his exit must have dissuaded him. He threw his hands into the air. "Look, I got sick that night. And your brother told me if I had to leave again not to bother coming back, so I didn't."

Stiller kept mentioning Grey's brother and Toni frowned in confusion. Grey never spoke about his family much, but it seemed odd that if the brothers worked together at the paper that talk about his presence wouldn't have come up during at least one of their conversations.

Grey kept his tone soft but she heard the edge of steel beneath. "Word's out that you just paid off half your marker. Where'd you get the cash?"

That Stiller had suddenly paid off gambling debts suggested he'd taken a bribe to sabotage those trucks. No doubt Grey wanted to know who'd hired the man.

"I won it."

Stiller didn't sound the least bit convincing.

"From whom?"

"I inherited it." Stiller changed his story, his gaze again shifting to the door. Sweat pooled under his armpits as he realized his mistake.

Not only was the man lacking intelligence, he was a poor liar. Even she could see Stiller hadn't the brains to have pulled off sabotaging those trucks without taking orders from someone.

But Grey fascinated her. He reminded her of a jungle cat, lean, honed and ready to pounce. His eyes reflected the thrill of the chase and anticipation in outing his foe.

And again she wondered why he'd brought her here.

"We can do this the hard way or the easy way. I understand you still have debts to cover." Grey pulled a stack of hundred-dollar bills from his pocket.

At the sight of the money, Stiller licked his lips. "If I didn't pay, they were going to break my legs. I wouldn't be able to work."

Grey fanned the money under Stiller's nose. "The interest on your debts is going up as we speak."

Stiller's shoulders sagged, but his eyes remained cagey, his tone shrewd. "What do you want?"

"A name. The person who hired you."

Before Stiller could answer, the eager waitress who knew Grey's favorite drink entered the room and shot Grey a knowing megawatt smile. "Would you like me to refresh your drink, Zane?"

Zane?

Who was Zane?

13

TONI'S FACE PALED AND her eyes rounded with shock as she stared at him accusingly. Although he'd planned for her to meet Stiller, he hadn't realized that the people in the casino might call him by name. His real name. Zane could have kicked himself for not recognizing the possibility. When in New Orleans, he frequented the casinos often, enjoying the nightlife and the action.

Now his past had come back to bite him big time. Only Toni was paying the price. He could see in the shock, disappointment and sadness in her eyes what his lies had cost her. The normal sparkle was gone and he had no one to blame but himself.

He ached to explain, to console her, but now was not the time. He squeezed her shoulder. "Just give me two more minutes with this piece of slime and then I'll explain."

Furious with Stiller for his traitorous activities as, Zane glared at the traitor. "Who paid you to—"

"If I tell you, I'm a dead man." Stiller's gaze went to the money. "As much as I could use the dough, I can't—"

"Boss," Zane's bodyguard spoke for the first time. "Leave me alone with him for five minutes, and I'll get you an answer. Those five minutes will be the longest of his life."

Stiller's face went as pale as Toni's. Zane let the silence drag out, suspecting the first man to talk would lose. Under normal circumstances he would hold out as long as it took. But he ached to make his explanation to Toni more than he wanted to find his saboteur. The longer he waited, the more time she would have to stew about how badly he'd treated her. Damn.

"A name, Stiller," Zane pressed.

"All I can say is that it's someone close to you."

Zane had no stomach for violence. He nodded to the bodyguard, wanting him to deal with the authorities and leave him free to make explanations to Toni. "Call the cops and tell them we caught the man responsible for damaging our trucks. I'll make a statement in the morning."

His chauffeur handed Zane the valet ticket. With a flick of the wrist, he closed his fingers about the paper, crunching it inside a tight fist. With the other hand, he reached for Toni. Her skin was as cold as ice, and he thought she might pull away from him. But she acted as though his touch was of no consequence to her whatsoever. His stomach tensed. He almost preferred she'd hit him, yell at him, anything to break into her damning withdrawal.

Holding her head high, she walked out of the casino without saying a word, totally ignoring him. He only hoped she was saving her anger for when they reached the sidewalk outside. Never had he seen anyone exhibit more control.

He wished she would release the pent-up anger. He didn't know how to read or cope with the ice queen she'd suddenly become. He supposed he deserved whatever angry words she threw at him and both guilt and remorse stabbed him. She was so self-contained and withdrawn that he wondered if she'd already figured out that he'd suspected her of complicity in the sabotage.

Stiller had said someone close to him was the traitor.

He could have lied. He could have meant Toni. Or he could have been referring to someone else.

In Zane's heart, he knew Toni had to be innocent. When she'd arrived at Grey's meeting in that gorilla suit and someone had poured oil in the ink, the timing had to be sheer happenstance. Her association with the senator, a man who had reason to hate the *Louisiana Daily Herald,* was likely just as she'd described it. That she had been with Zane at Club Carnal while Stiller had sabotaged the trucks had to be another fluke. And her access to the computer before someone had altered the headlines had been simple bad luck.

If only they'd met under other circumstances. He tossed the valet a twenty-dollar bill.

At least someone was happy. The valet tipped his hat with a wide grin. "I'll be right back, sir."

Zane and Toni stood together on the sidewalk, but he couldn't have felt more alone. "Say something," he pleaded.

"I must have been an idiot to think I'd fallen in love with a man who didn't trust me enough to tell me his name. His real name. Goodbye, Zane."

She headed toward a taxi, her back straight. Her words struck him like a brutal right hook to the temple. She'd thought she loved him? And she'd said the words in the past tense as if he'd killed that emotion. Other women had told them they'd loved him and he'd known he'd stayed too long and had run away. But now all he felt was this huge ball of guilt roiling in his stomach. Usually with Zane, what a woman saw was what she got, a good time. He made no bones that he was a party animal. But he'd lied to her by misrepresenting himself, his character, his intentions.

He hurried to her side. "I'm sorry. Please. Let me explain."

She spun on her heel. "You're an identical twin?"

"Yes."

At his admission, she looked as though she couldn't decide whether to hit him, berate him or ignore him. All because of his deceit. The man she'd just made love to had lied to her about his name. Guilt sliced him. "And you're Zane? Not Grey?"

"Yes."

"Why did you lie to me?"

"We agreed to switch places *before* you and I ever met."

"You hadn't changed places yet when I wore the gorilla suit to the newspaper?"

"No," he answered, wondering why she'd asked, but not caring as long as she kept speaking to him, giving him a chance to explain. "Grey needed a vacation and I offered to try and figure out who was sabotaging the company while he took some much needed R and R."

"And the reason you lied and didn't tell me your name was because—"

"I didn't tell anyone," he said quickly, not wanting to admit his reasons. Like that he suspected she was the saboteur. But the stark pain in her eyes told him she'd already figured it out.

"You thought I had something to do with your problems, didn't you?" Her tone was like a soft glove over steel. Obviously the hurt was still there, but her anger had begun to erect a barrier between them.

"There were too many coincidences not to think that your involvement was a possibility," he admitted.

"What coincidences?"

"You were with me at Club Carnal during the time Stiller damaged the trucks. You had access to the computer when the headlines were altered. And you neglected to tell me of your involvement with the senator."

Surely she could understand that his suspicions were reasonable?

"And those suspicions didn't stop you from screwing me, did they?"

Her use of the vulgarity not only shocked him, it made him realize just how deeply he'd hurt her. She felt used and he couldn't blame her. But being with her hadn't been like that for him. "We were making love."

"Were we?"

"When we were together, I didn't think you were guilty."

"How convenient."

She hammered him with words more devastating than a prizefighter's punches, each reply jabbing him, bruising, cutting, slicing and dicing him into little pieces. Backed into a corner of his own making, he had no place to go, no way to escape.

He tried again. "Making love to you was special. You are special."

"You've done nothing but lie to me since we've met. Why should I believe you now?" She threaded her fingers through her hair, then tossed her locks over her shoulder. "Hell, Zane, Stiller told you that your traitor is someone close to you. It could be me."

"It's not."

"But you don't know for sure, do you? I'll prove my innocence to you, and then you'll never have to see me again."

She was going to leave him—but not yet. That meant he still had time with her, time to get her to change her mind.

She was too angry for him to argue with now, so he simply asked, "What do you want me to do?"

"We're going to set a trap."

TONI HAD NEVER WANTED TO hit a man in her life. But she wanted to pound her fists on Zane's chest, scream in his face, kick him in the shins. But even if she acted out her rage, she couldn't make him feel as though his insides had been torn to shreds and left to blow in the wind, tattered, torn, bloody.

Anger helped her deal with the hurt. Anger kept her going, kept back the tears that tightened her throat, constricted her heart and stung her pride. How could she not have seen that he had no feelings for her? Oh, sure, they had sexual chemistry. No big deal. German shepherds in heat had chemistry. Siamese cats had chemistry.

Hormones.

Pheromones.

Lust.

He had slept with her, lied to her, caused her to fall in love with him, and she hated that he could have twisted such good emotions into memories that made her ashamed, not of the sex, but of her judgment. How could she have been so wrong about him? Why hadn't she suspected that he couldn't trust her? That he couldn't be trusted?

Because he was good at his lies.

Even now as they hid together in the pressroom closet, their bodies occasionally brushing against one another, she felt the connection. Not that she would acknowledge her body's betrayal. Just because he'd conditioned her to become aroused by his presence didn't mean she wanted him ever again. Okay, she *did* want him, but her anger was still way stronger than desire.

They would catch his saboteur. Her plan had been simple. Zane had called an emergency meeting of the heads of every department. He'd explained that the *Louisiana Daily Herald* had won a ten-page advertisement that would announce plans for a new mall, hotel and casino. The consortium planned to keep advertising with his paper and only his paper, but it was critical that nothing went wrong with tonight's run.

He'd fabricated the entire story and secretly pulled the faked ads himself at the last minute. Tomorrow's paper wouldn't include the ten pages of advertisements. However, since Toni had asked Zane to make a huge deal about it, she hoped the saboteur would show up and attempt to stop the presses.

"I hope Grey's people bought my little act," Zane muttered.

"I'm sure they did. You're a very good liar."

He placed a hand on her arm, tentatively. "I never meant to hurt you."

"I know." But he *had* hurt her and they both knew it.

She would recover from the hurt. What bothered her was that she no longer trusted her judgment. Perhaps she was one of those career women who would end up without a lifetime partner. It wouldn't be the end of the world. She had her career, her family, her friends.

She would go on and put Zane behind her. She would allow herself time to mourn the loss and she would move forward. She would be fine.

On the other hand, she wasn't so sure about Zane. He didn't seem like the same carefree and playful man she'd once known. The lightness had disappeared from his step. His easy grin looked forced. But tomorrow night, he'd probably console himself with a night on the town with some bimbo, while, in spite of herself, she worried about him.

She felt sorry that he was so clueless about his feelings for her that he was willing to let her go. But she didn't feel guilty for messing up his perfect playboy world and could only hope that maybe he would come to realize that he did care for her.

She peered through the closet door slats, unwilling to look in Zane's direction. The press seemed to run normally. The men running the machines worked with a casual efficiency.

Maybe the saboteur wouldn't take the bait. She bent her neck to her shoulder in an attempt to work out a crick.

Zane immediately placed his hands on her shoulders and began to massage the sore muscle.

She stepped back. "Don't."

The tension between them couldn't have been thicker, but as much as she wanted to pretend that his touch meant nothing to her, she couldn't.

"I don't know what words to say to make this better," he muttered. "But if you just tell me, I'll say them."

She steeled herself against his obvious remorse. "Words can't always fix what's wrong."

They went back to another uncomfortable silence.

Watching the pressroom. Looking for anything suspicious.

"There." Zane put his hands on her shoulders and turned her toward the far wall.

"I see only dark shadows."

"Keep looking. Let your eyes adjust."

"There's a man."

"Yep."

"Now what?" Her scheme hadn't gone any further than getting the saboteur to reveal himself. Still, satisfaction swept through her. Zane could no longer have even the slightest suspicion that she was a criminal. Although he never thought she'd committed the dirty work, only been the distraction, if she had been guilty, she would never have helped point out the real culprit.

"We wait until he causes damage. I want to catch him in the act."

"How?"

Zane took his cell phone out of his pocket and dialed 911. The presses seemed to grow louder in volume and she couldn't hear his words, until he turned and ordered her, "Stay here."

How just like a man. Accuse her. Betray her trust. Then use her plan, and when it works, tell her to stay back. She didn't think so.

As soon as Zane exited the closet, she followed, curious to see whose face would emerge from the darkness. Besides, she wanted the satisfaction of seeing Zane's face when he finally realized that she had nothing to do with his problems—at least not the ones at the paper.

Zane moved in an unhurried fashion. She had no trouble keeping up with him and he couldn't hear her following, thanks to the noise of the presses.

They were within about ten feet of the intruder when Zane flicked on additional lights. Lights that revealed a man prying open the electric box with a pair of wire cutters, no doubt intent on shutting down the entire electric system and thereby halting the presses.

"Turn around," Zane ordered.

Instead of obeying the command, the intruder threw the cutters in their direction. Zane ducked, she shifted behind a pallet of cartons. She saw now that he should have notified security or his bodyguard. But fearful of leaks, Zane had insisted he could handle the intruder alone.

And when Zane raced after the man, she sprinted behind him, keeping up as best she could. Up a flight of steps. Through a heavy doorway. Down a hallway. Several yards ahead of her, Zane tackled the man from behind and the two rolled across the floor, each of them flailing for a grip on the other. Elbows and knees slammed into flesh.

When Toni caught up, she snatched up a potted plant and drew closer, waiting for an opportunity to help Zane. She never planned to see him again after tonight, but she wouldn't let the saboteur kill him. When the two men rolled in her direction, she slammed the pot into the stranger's head.

Zane was breathing heavily. "I think you got him. Thanks, but didn't I tell you to stay—"

"Who is he?" Toni asked.

Zane turned him over and the man's eyes fluttered open just as the police arrived. "Stephen."

Grey's right-hand man? He'd certainly had the means and opportunity to damage the paper. But what had been his motive?

"Why?" Zane asked.

"Grey was going to fire me."

As the man revealed his betrayal of Zane's twin, she read anger and hurt in Zane's expression. And for the tiniest moment his reaction weakened her resolve. But she hardened her heart.

"You did this for revenge?"

Stephen shook his head. "I wouldn't have done any real damage. I just wanted to prove to Grey that he needed me. When I realized you two had switched places, I figured it was an opportunity to increase my activity."

So Stephen had been aware of the switch all along. "You don't call putting sand in the truck's gas tanks or oil in the ink real damage?"

"The Mastersons can afford a few losses. And with you so distracted by the new woman in your life, you never even thought to suspect me."

Stephen hadn't framed her—not exactly. He'd simply used her time with Zane to do his mischief, making her appear guilty.

Zane picked Stephen up from the floor and shoved him toward the cops. "My brother doesn't need his kind of help. Take him downtown. We intend to press charges."

The cops handcuffed Stephen and read him his rights. Zane gave them a short statement. Toni did the same.

Then she walked out of the building and didn't look back. Tears rained down her cheeks when Zane didn't even make an effort to stop her. Not that he could have stopped her.

But, damn him, he didn't even try.

ZANE SPENT THE NEXT week assuring himself that he would get over Toni Maxwell. So what if his stomach felt as if it were filled with rocks? So what if every time he went out, he kept hoping he might bump into her? So what if she'd spoiled other women for him? So what if he couldn't go back to his normal schedule, his usual way of thinking?

Not that he hadn't tried. He'd resorted to taking an old flame to the casinos. Even a huge run of luck at the crap tables hadn't distracted him from his misery. Neither had a one-night drinking binge. He'd even taken a businesswoman friend clubbing. The woman was friendly, intelligent, pleasant and a knockout, but he left her at her front door with a kiss on the forehead and a heavy heart.

Women didn't do this to him. Women didn't dump him. Women didn't make him feel low. And he wasn't about to let it get to him. But Toni Maxwell *had* gotten to him in a way he didn't want to acknowledge or even think about. When fifty-yard-line seats at the Saints-Rams game didn't pull him out of the doldrums, he knew he was in trouble. Maybe he was coming down with a cold or the flu. Finally he admitted he simply had to give himself time to recover from Toni's effect on him.

A week simply must not be long enough to get over a woman. Still, a tiny voice niggled at the back of his mind. He still had his freedom, which he valued most, but what good was freedom if he wasn't happy?

He'd always smirked in superiority at other men in his condition, believing they were fools for letting a woman under their skin. And now he thought himself a fool. But he'd get over her. Forget her.

At night, she haunted his dreams, and he woke up aroused and aching for her, recalling her bright laughter, the way she liked to have fun, the way she made him feel good, happy, eager to face the day.

As opposed to how he felt now. Moody. Somber. On edge. Fighting gloom and melancholy.

A week later, he threw himself into work, telling himself that an occupied mind would get him over the mourning period faster. This plan also failed.

He paced, wearing a path in Grey's carpet, stared at the phone for hours, and when he got her machine and left a message, she didn't return his calls. He kept checking his watch. Why? He didn't know. He kept checking the phone to make sure the line was working.

When he finally broke down and phoned her shop, he was told she didn't wish to speak to him. He sent flowers, and she refused them. And when, in desperation, he knocked on her front door, one of her sisters told him that she didn't want to see him.

And that was when he realized that he was in trouble. Deep, sinking trouble. No woman had ever refused him. Telling himself Toni's reaction was his own fault did no good. Who cared whose fault it was? Casting blame only made him seem pathetic. Instead, he would think about what he could do now. What he wanted now.

He wanted her back. Had to see her and straighten out this mess. But he couldn't talk to her when she wouldn't answer her phone or come to her door.

He considered going to her shop, but he didn't want to meet her on her own turf where her sisters could have him thrown out. And then one day while he was shaving, he looked at himself in the mirror. He had dark circles under his eyes from brooding and from a lack of sleep. His face was grim, his lips tight, his skin unhealthy looking.

He considered a change of scenery. Europe could be pleasant in the fall. He could sail in New Zealand or surf Oahu's north shore or scuba dive the Great Barrier Reef or hunt pheasant in South Dakota. But nothing appealed to him. Not even a photographic safari in Kenya.

And that was when he knew that something was very wrong with him. As much as he'd tried to deny it, he had uncontrollable feelings for Toni Maxwell. As the abhorrent thought that he had fallen for her hit him, he nicked his face shaving. Blood trickled from the cut, spattered in his sink. With a vicious twist of the faucet, he washed away the blood, wishing he could wash away his feelings.

Damn it. He hadn't planned to fall in love.

He liked his life just the way it was, thank you very much. He didn't intend to change his freedom-loving spirit for any woman, especially not someone who wouldn't take his phone calls. Especially not for a woman who wouldn't see his side of things. Especially not a woman with such high standards.

Okay, so he had fallen in love. He was human. He would forgive himself the weakness and get over it.

But as he entered week three, with next-to-no sleep and having dropped another five pounds, he decided to reassess. Living his life alone and his way was making him miserable. Freedom no longer seemed so wonderful. His normally fulfilling activities seemed empty. With the newspaper running smoothly, he was bored, the routine seemed draining.

But he liked the sense of self-accomplishment he'd achieved from turning things around. He'd found he had a knack for the publishing business. He enjoyed solving the difficulties, but the day-to-day responsibilities bored him. With Stephen behind bars and awaiting trial, and the newspaper's circulation up, Zane considered expanding the paper across the state. However, he wanted to talk to Grey, but his brother had been incommunicado since Stephen's arrest, and Zane, who'd never bothered his brother with his problems before, wasn't about to start now.

A challenge would be good for him. He enjoyed solving problems. Too bad he couldn't set his own life to rights so easily.

By the end of the third week as he tossed and turned alone in bed, he'd decided that he wasn't getting over Toni. He missed her. Obviously, she wasn't going to change her mind about him—unless he did something drastic. But drastic meant that *he* would have to change. Permanently.

Restless, he kicked the covers off his feet. Why the hell should he offer to give up his precious freedom and change his life for her?

Because he was miserable without her. Because if he didn't at least try to get her back, he'd never forgive himself.

He punched his pillow. Yes, he was Zane—the freewheeling bachelor who avoided responsibilities. But admitting that he might want a more committed lifestyle didn't mean he was giving up his identity.

Bingo!

All his life, Zane had thought of himself as the free spirit, the laid-back and independent one, the fun twin. But just because he might want to settle down with Toni, maybe raise a few kids, didn't mean he was some inferior shadow of Grey, the responsible one. If he married Toni, he would still be Zane. He could still have fun.

Marry?

Why was he even thinking about marriage when she wouldn't even talk to him? He must be losing his mind to consider tying himself to a woman who wouldn't accept his apology.

He had treated her badly.

But he'd lied to her before he'd known he loved her. While he supposed he should have recognized his symptoms sooner, why would he? He'd never been in love before.

Okay, he loved her. Admitting it to himself had yet to kill him. He was still Zane, just a Zane who loved a woman. He could wrap his mind around it. Zane loved Toni Maxwell. Okay.

He turned on his back, laced his fingers behind his head and stared at the ceiling.

Go with the flow. Use the knowledge.

She'd also admitted that she'd loved him.

Good. Good.

And recent experience had taught him that stopping these strong kinds of feelings was next to impossible. He'd certainly tried, and failed.

Where was he going with this?

Perhaps she had been just as unsuccessful. After all, if her feelings for him hadn't been so strong, he wouldn't have been able to hurt her so badly, he realized with sickening clarity. Why were his thoughts so clear, now, after he'd done so much damage?

However, Zane wasn't much into remorse and regret. He much preferred to focus on rectifying his mistakes. What was he going to do? Now that he knew his goal—winning her back—he needed a plan.

He loved her.

He wanted the freedom to love her.

He'd already tried flowers and phone calls and showing up at her door. She wasn't ready to forgive and forget, but he refused to face the possibility that she never would.

Deciding to take matters into his own hands, he'd cleared his path for action. One phone call to Birdstrum had accomplished his task. If Birdstrum didn't back off from Toni, or if he fired her father or messed with her sisters, Zane would expose the senator's sexual preferences on page one. Birdstrum, ahead in the polls, had caved, leaving Zane free to reclaim his woman's affections.

Zane knew how to charm women. He knew how to chase them and seduce them. Surely he could come up with a scheme to win her back.

Would Toni go for the grand gesture? A spectacular gesture?

And did he dare risk the humiliation of the very possible chance that she would refuse any overtures he made?

Zane grinned, leaped out of bed and headed to the kitchen, hungry for the first time in weeks.

14

"TONI, YOU AREN'T GOING to believe this." Bobby slapped the newspaper down on the kitchen table, almost knocking over a pitcher of orange juice.

"Oh, my." Jude peered over Bobby's shoulder but Toni refused to look at the front page of the *Louisiana Daily Herald.* And she would continue to listen to her news on the radio until she could read a paper without thinking about Zane. The playful smile and his deceitful style may have done a number on her, but she was determined to put her mistake behind her. Reading his new daily columns about the upcoming elections, or the "Hot Scoops" column, wouldn't help her cause. Sure she still loved him, even understood why he'd acted the way he had, but that didn't make her hurt any less. If he had feelings for her, he would have told her the truth, at least his real name, before they'd made love.

And that was how she thought of their time together—as loving. She had loved him. Just the thought of him still caused her breath to hitch in her chest and her heart to start its own tap dance across her ribs.

Mickey stopped flipping bacon long enough to look at the paper and gasp. "Zane Masterson must be insane."

Ever since Zane had lied to Toni, she'd no interest in his newspaper, his "Hot Scoops" column or in him.

In fact, she'd considered canceling his paper and ordering a competitor's, but she couldn't bring herself to do it.

"Zane doesn't look insane to me." Bobby sighed dramatically. "He looks hot."

Mickey frowned. "Bobby!"

"Well, he does," she insisted as she bit her lip and smudged pink lipstick on her teeth.

"Toni can't ignore him now," Jude muttered with dreamy satisfaction.

"Sure I can." Defiantly, Toni slathered strawberry preserves on her English muffin and refused to look at Zane's column. "If he had any sense, he would have canceled that 'Hot Scoops' column."

Bobby thrust the paper between the English muffin and Toni's mouth. "Does this look like a measly column to you? It looks like the entire front page to me."

Toni dropped the English muffin and stared at the picture of Zane on his knees. Zane on his knees in a tuxedo with an open jewelry box that showed a plain gold wedding band. What the hell was he doing on his knees? When she could finally tear her gaze from the compelling picture, her eyes strayed upward to the four-inch headline. "Marry Me, Toni."

"This has to be a joke. Like printing a sweetheart's name on the cover of a fake *Vogue* magazine. Zane certainly has the resources to print a phony newspaper." How dare he mock her, make fun of her like this. Toni shoved the paper aside. "It's a fake, a mockup that he had delivered just to us."

Bobby shook her head, her eyes amused yet sympathetic. "I considered that, so I walked to the corner newsstand. The same headline and photograph are on every copy. Our neighbors have them, too. It's for real, all right.''

''I don't believe it.'' Toni stared at the paper, unsure whether to laugh or to cry as his outrageous gesture began to sink in. Not that Zane was a private, shy man, but, still, he had been willing to make a public spectacle of himself for her. The thought was flattering.

She'd always wanted the right man to propose to her. Just not so publicly. What had he been thinking?

''He wants to marry you,'' Jude insisted.

Bobby read over her shoulder. ''He has the wedding planned for tomorrow afternoon.''

''Five o'clock,'' Jude said.

This couldn't be happening. Denial wanted to set in but her sisters kept jabbering excitedly.

Mickey's voice rose a notch. ''He's going to wait for you in Jackson Square.''

''How romantic,'' Bobby cooed.

How utterly ridiculous, Toni thought. And ironic. Zane was doing precisely what Birdstrum had done—and, thankfully, had stopped doing—trying to force her into marriage.

Only this time, she loved the man.

''We haven't even spoken to one another in almost a month.''

Mickey chuckled. ''Apparently, he missed you.''

''Very funny.'' Toni couldn't seem to think with any kind of logic. What was with these men who kept trying to force her into marriage? She and Zane had had something special together, but she was still angry with him. And she didn't trust him, didn't trust her judgment after mistaking his character so badly. Her fingers itched to shred the newspaper and burn it. Pretend she'd never received a copy. She wondered why the phone wasn't ringing and glanced over to see that one of her sisters had already taken it off the hook.

"Zane Masterson's invited the entire city to witness your wedding ceremony," Jude read slowly.

The doorbell rang insistently. "Don't answer it," Toni ordered in a panic, her stomach roiling in turmoil. "I don't want to talk to anyone."

"It's not just anyone. I called in reinforcements." Mickey ignored her baffled look and stepped to the front door. "Hi Mom. Dad. Glad you could make it."

Clearly, Mickey had stepped in and decided to get their parents involved. Likely, they knew all the details by now.

"How is she?" Their mother rushed into the room, her eyes full of concern and wrapped her arms around Toni, who suddenly wanted to burst into tears. Instead she just hugged her mom, then her dad, swallowing the burning lump in her throat.

Her father patted her shoulder, his twinkling blue eyes serious but kind. His blond hair had long ago turned to a distinguished gray, a perfect complement to her mother's dark auburn, cut short in the latest style. Her mother might have taught Toni about fashion, but her dad was the one she'd talked to about her goals and dreams.

He tugged her back into her chair, then took the seat opposite and leaned forward intently. "So tell us what's in your heart."

"I don't know."

"She loves him," her mother said. "I can see it in her face."

"Sometimes love isn't enough," Toni told them wearily, the excitement of the last few minutes sapping her energy. "Especially when that love is one-sided."

"Are you nuts?" Bobby thrust the paper back into her hands. "He loves you. He says so right here. Page one. Paragraph three. Line five."

"That's news to me."

"Honey," her mother helped herself to a cup of coffee, "he's obviously crazy about you."

"He lied to me."

"So get over it." Jude sighed. "The man's put a picture of himself on his knees and publicly proposed and declared his love for you in front of the entire city."

"What else could he possibly do to say he's sorry?" Mickey asked softly.

"Or to prove he loves you?" Bobby added.

Toni understood all too well why he'd lied to her. In his eyes, she'd appeared guilty of sabotage, especially since Stephen had used her presence to his advantage. Given the circumstances, he couldn't have trusted her. And if he couldn't trust her, he shouldn't have made love to her. But how could he resist—when she couldn't resist him, either?

In a way, his inability to resist making love to her when he didn't trust her was a compliment. And an indication of the strong, undeniable connection between them. So, yes, he'd lied to her…but she forgave him.

Her father took her hand. "While I appreciate your efforts on my behalf, did you really think I'd work for a man who would blackmail my daughter?"

"You quit?" Her heart pounded with pride.

He nodded. "And found another job. So you have no fear of Birdstrum's backlash against me. You have only yourself to consider. What does your heart say?"

"My heart says to marry him—"

"Then do it," Bobby urged.

"But I'm still hurt by his deception."

Her father entwined his fingers in hers. "You shouldn't marry a man that you can't forgive."

"Wrong," her mother disagreed. "She's hurting because she loves him. She's still angry because she loves him. A woman can hold anger and love in her heart. But how's this for a plan? Set those conflicting emotions aside for the wedding day. Save them for the wedding night."

"Mom!" Mickey exclaimed.

"Mother!" Bobby squealed.

"Now I've really heard more than I needed to hear." Toni squeezed her father's hand, then withdrew it and stood. "If you all don't mind, I have some thinking to do."

Toni paced her room. During this last month she'd missed Zane terribly. His aptitude for grand gestures made her smile and want to cry all at the same time. What a mess.

Had Toni changed? What had happened to the reckless risk taker who had started up a business with only one month's capital? What had happened to the reckless woman who'd set out to create a sex scandal? Where was she now when Toni needed her?

To marry a man like Zane took courage. The man could be kind and infuriating. His lovemaking was the best she'd ever had. She loved him. But marriage? Tomorrow? Her mouth turned dry as desert sand. But she enjoyed his company more than anyone's she'd ever met.

So why did her knees shake so much she wanted to lie down? Why did she feel as if she stood unbalanced and unhinged on the edge of a sharp precipice? Would leaping toward Zane be foolish? Insane?

Would stepping back to regain her footing be the biggest mistake of her life?

ZANE WAITED IN Jackson Square, wondering if he'd ever recover from so public a humiliation if Toni didn't show up. He'd deliberately removed his watch and placed it in his pocket in order not to be seen checking it every ten seconds. With the late-afternoon sun casting golden rays over the crowded square, he tried not to crane his neck to search for Toni, tried not to shift from foot to foot.

The crowd, a mixture of curious tourists, friends and business associates, milled in the square, his brother, Grey, among them. Their parents wouldn't make it back from their travels, but considering the bride might not show, Zane would have felt guilty for interrupting their trip.

Toni still hadn't communicated with him. Not by a note, a phone call. Not even an e-mail. If this was her way of taking her revenge, he supposed he deserved it. However, he still kept hoping that she would accept his oh-so-public proposal. Surely if she loved him, she would forgive him?

He had plane tickets for their honeymoon in Tahiti in his coat pocket, one of those tiki huts on stilts over the water reserved in their names. Mr. and Mrs. Zane Masterson had a ring to it that he liked.

Speaking of rings. He jammed his hand into his pocket and plucked out the plain gold band that had been his grandmother's. If Toni wanted, she could pick out an engagement ring later. But this ring was his grandmother's and she had enjoyed a lasting marriage.

He knew a ring didn't make a good marriage—but hey, what could using the same ring hurt?

He couldn't bring himself to believe that she wouldn't come. Didn't want to face that kind of pain.

Grey joined him at the front gate where Zane kept a lookout. "How're you holding up?"

"I've been better."

Grey gestured to the paparazzi. "You want me to talk to the mayor about banishing those reporters?"

Zane forced a grin. "Now how would it look for the owner of the *Louisiana Daily Herald* to ban the press from a public square?"

Grey chuckled. "Who cares?"

Zane turned and stared at the face that mirrored his own. Grey had never looked more relaxed. The shadows in his eyes were gone as his brother's hungry gaze followed a dark-haired voluptuous woman—Reina Price, the erotic jewelry artist. Was she the reason that light had chased away the shadows in his brother's eyes?

Before he could comment or observe further, a horse-drawn carriage pulled up and stopped at the square's open gates. Toni, her eyes seeking Zane's, her white gown a vision of cream satin and lace that showed off her smooth skin, sat still as stone, her hands clutching a bouquet of daisies.

Her sisters gaily stepped out of the carriage, leaving her alone. Unable to wait another moment, Zane hoisted himself up. He noted that two people who he suspected were her parents, exited a taxi behind them.

Although dozens of cameras flashed in their direction, for a moment, they had a semblance of privacy. His mouth went dry and he suddenly didn't know what to say.

Toni turned to him, her eyes flashing with warmth, banked hunger and perhaps a touch of trepidation. "Hi."

"Hi, yourself." Damn, this was awkward. But Zane knew how to put everything right. He leaned forward, dipping his head to hers. Another woman might fuss that her groom was about to mess up her makeup, but Toni wound her arms around his neck and raised her head to meet him.

Her lips parted beneath his, soft and welcoming. She pressed close to him and he revelled in her scent, in the eagerness of her lips. When the reporters started to move in, breaking the moment, he instinctively tried to shelter her.

"What made you say yes, Ms. Maxwell?" called out one reporter.

"When did you know you loved him?" shouted another.

"Do you have any doubts?"

"Where are you going on your honeymoon?"

"Are you pregnant?"

Zane felt her stiffen at the last hurled question. She pulled back a little and whispered. "Do you want children, Zane?"

"I don't hate them. I've never thought about..."

She chuckled. "I have a feeling there're a lot of things you haven't thought about." Her face turned more serious. "Maybe we're rushing things."

"I love you. The rest is all details."

"I love you, too, but we've never talked about a future together. Where we'll live..."

"We'll live wherever you want. How's New Orleans sound? I hear it's a party town and a good place to run a business."

She raised an eyebrow. "Zane, you have quite the jet-set reputation. You won't feel tied down? You won't get bored?"

"Not with you. Never with you. Before I was alone in a crowd. With you, I don't feel alone. I feel whole. Complete. Happy."

"For how long?"

"The nomadic lifestyle isn't all it's cracked up to be." He shrugged again. "And whenever we want, I'll sweep you away to Fiji or Nevis or the dry Tortugas."

"All islands."

"How do you feel about a honeymoon in Tahiti?"

"How do you feel about spending the rest of your life with one woman?"

"Lucky. Very lucky." She looked so good that he ached to take her onto his lap and hold her, just to savor the feel of her in his arms. He'd missed her terribly these last few weeks, but until now he hadn't realized how much. His spirit lifted just at the sight of her tender smile. A smile that was all for him, even while being captured by dozens of cameras.

"I've arranged for a judge to marry us and I want you to introduce me to your parents." He realized in his happiness that he was practically babbling, closed his mouth and helped her from the carriage while strangers and friends let out a cheer. The bride blushed, her eyes sparkling.

She introduced him to her parents who seemed like nice people, especially under the circuslike circumstances. And then the wedding music started, her father placed Toni's hand in his and together they walked toward the judge.

Zane barely heard the judge utter the short civil ceremony. He kept his gaze on Toni, realizing he was a lucky man to have found her. Although he'd arranged for a photographer, he wanted to memorize the moment, savor their happiness. And when he placed his grandmother's ring on her finger and waited impatiently for another kiss, he knew he could look forward to a lifetime of Toni's kisses. And that whatever future they chose would be wonderful because they would share their lives. Forever.

* * * * *

Don't miss the exciting story of
Zane's twin in
DOUBLE THE PLEASURE
by Julie Elizabeth Leto.
On shelves now!

Turn the page for a sneak preview….

1

"I'M HERE," SHE CALLED, poking her head through the doorway.

"I know, but dinner's down here."

Zane marched up the staircase, the atmosphere in the cramped hallway altering the minute he came into view. He really was incredibly gorgeous, Reina thought. Deep-set, thoughtful blue eyes. Soft, wavy hair—a little shorter than he normally wore it, but still begging to be combed by a woman's fingers. And his smile. Always tilted to that one angle that made her wonder exactly what he found so amusing.

Only Zane's smile didn't seem too lopsided tonight. His grin held a tinge of something Reina might best describe as tentative. Wary, even.

A shiver shot up her spine, but she didn't know if the reaction resulted from the difference in Zane's expression or the fact that he'd fully entered her personal space, his shoulder pressed against her doorjamb, his face inches from hers.

"Aren't you hungry?"

He poured a generous ounce of sexual innuendo into his question, snapping Reina back into her protective persona. She licked her lips, then stepped back to blatantly check him out. "Starved, actually."

He slipped his hand around hers. "Come with me, then."

"I don't want to leave my—" she paused, eyeing Brandon at work across the hall, "—treasures unguarded."

Zane lobbed his own appreciative glance down her torso. "No, we can't have that." He nodded toward her bedroom. "If you'll allow me, I can show you how we can alleviate your problem."

Reina bit the inside of her mouth to keep from grinning. This flirtation thing could be a lot of fun, particularly since she knew he was only toying with her because he could. She did know that, right? She used to know that. She and Zane had played attentive lovers at parties on several occasions, mainly to amuse their crowd and keep matchmaking friends from attempting a fix-up. Their feigned sexual attraction had always been a private joke between them.

Right?

Zane pulled her inside and quietly closed the door. He looked around the room, nodding, but saying nothing.

"What?" she asked.

He cleared his throat. "I'm just trying to remember what the room looked like before you redecorated."

Reina had to think herself. Redecorating the bedroom had been her first project. "The walls were chintz. Roses, I think."

Zane nodded. "Yes, *grand-mère* did love florals. Do you remember where the bed was?"

Reina closed her eyes. She knew she'd moved the bed, having immediately thought Zane's great-grandmother had it in a strange place, partially blocking a window. "Over there."

Zane followed Reina's instructions to the window Brandon had just wired, then walked five paces toward the wall. About halfway down, he tapped the wall with his fist. The sound was hard and thick. He adjusted an inch and knocked again. This time, the sound echoed.

Instantly, with a mechanical grunt, a panel of the wall slipped aside.

"Wha—?"

Zane grinned. "Apparently, I never told you about some of the special features of this old house."

Reina scurried to the opening, stepping back when a ripe, musty smell assailed her. She grabbed a large, lit, scented candle and thrust it into the narrow opening. The flame flickered, but remained steady as fresh air seeped inside. The room, a closet really, barely had enough space for anyone to stand fully upright.

"Extra storage space?" she asked.

Zane took the candle. "Not quite."

He leaned into the darkness and tapped the inner wall. Another panel slid aside. Stale air crept out, tickling her nostrils so that she nearly sneezed.

"Another room?" Reina guessed, grabbing a tissue from the box on her dresser.

"There are several," Zane told her. "Most of them are on the bottom floor, but this floor and the attic each have one and a passageway leading to the others. *Grand-mère* claimed they were used by the Underground Railroad to hide escaped slaves until they could be smuggled out on Yankee ships. My brother and I used to play one wicked game of hide-and-seek in this house."

"Who else knows about these rooms?" Reina retrieved the candle from him and ventured inside. In Europe, she'd always been fascinated by the castles and ancient architecture and, as a child, had been notorious for slipping away from the docent to explore on her own. New Orleans, with all its dark and devious history, held a similar appeal. She hadn't had much time to delve into the city's many mysteries since she'd moved to the area, and never would have guessed she had something so interesting in her own house.

"My brother, of course. My father, probably, though I'd bet he's long forgotten. His mother didn't get on well with *grand-mère*. He didn't spend a lot of time here in his youth."

She stepped across something sticky and silky, and swiped the web away. "You think it's safe to hide the jewels here?"

"I think it's safe enough for you to work in here. You can't tell now, but during the day, this particular room has good light from a window hidden by the eaves."

"It'll be hot," she said.

"Isn't it always when you're working?" Zane chuckled and Reina wished she hadn't chosen that exact phrasing. "I can rig a cooling unit. There's an old one in the garage that might still work."

Reina thrust her hand into the darkness, allowing the candle to throw uncertain light on the interior room, empty except for a few old crates and decades' worth of dust. She'd have some serious cleaning to do before she could set up shop, but if Zane helped, she could begin work on the collection by tomorrow afternoon. She nodded, silently agreeing that the room would work. She hadn't liked the idea of having to lock up the jewels each time she left her studio, maybe just to run to the bathroom or to grab something to drink. Now, with Zane in the house, the secret room, and Brandon's security system protecting the perimeter, she felt confident she could work without fear.

She eased back out of the tight space, startled when Zane blocked her retreat into her bedroom. The candlelight flickered as she pulled up short just a few inches from Zane's chest.

"Perfect, don't you agree?" he asked.

She glanced over her shoulder into the darkness. "Should have enough space and if the light is what you promise..."

"I always fulfill my promises."

Reina gulped in the musty air, the taste bitter. What was up with Zane, anyway? He was pouring it on a little thick, even for him. Or maybe he always flirted like this and, under normal circumstances, she rebuffed him without a second thought. That was, to some extent, a game they played—though usually not in private. Alone, Reina and Zane established a safe zone, a reserve where each of them could exist without having to worry about what the other might be thinking, might be wanting. Still, with Reina growing increasingly bored with the endless party scene, she couldn't remember the last time they'd been together. And something in their established dynamic had definitely changed.

"You don't usually make promises, Zane."

For a moment, his expression faltered. His ultimate Zane cockiness dropped away, and a flash of uncertainty sped through his eyes before he blew out the candle, dousing them in darkness. He folded his large body out of the secret passage and back into her bedroom.

"No promises. A fine way to keep from ever disappointing anyone."

He took her hand and helped her out, but released her fingers the minute she stepped clear. Reina noted his silence, wondering how he could support his theory about making no promises when he had so many broken hearts littering the path of his love life.

She shook her head. "Is that your secret?"

"I don't have any secrets," he said, his gaze focused somewhere, anywhere, other than directly on hers. "Not any good ones, anyway."

Reina retrieved the metal briefcase, which he slid into the passage before knocking the wall and closing the panel. She waited right next to him, demanding his attention by not moving out of his personal space, just like he'd done to her a moment ago. "I don't know. These secret rooms are pretty handy."

"I'm nothing if not handy."

Reina blew out a contemplative whistle, but didn't say another word until she'd crossed the room and opened the door into the hall. She spared a glance at the lump in her comforter, the hiding place of Viviana's diary, then at the space beneath her bed where she stored her collection of sex toys and pleasure aids. She couldn't remember the last time she'd used any of the ones intended for couples, nor could she remember ever doubting that satisfying herself would relieve her sexual anxiety.

After reading il Gio's diary last night, she'd indulged in an hour's worth of self-induced pleasure, starting with a long hot bath and ending with a rather intense orgasm. But now, with the combined thrill of embarking on a new project and confronting Zane's suddenly potent masculine charm, she was convinced that some steamy water and even a dildo weren't going to put a dent in squelching her libido tonight.

No, for that, she'd need a flesh-and-blood man.